The
Life
and Death of
Liam Faulds

The
Life
and Death of
Liam Faulds

a novel by
Hugh McLeave

ST. MARTIN'S PRESS / NEW YORK

Design by Manny Paul
Copy Editor: Nancy Mackenzie

Library of Congress Cataloging in Publication Data

McLeave, Hugh.
   The life and death of Liam Faulds.

"A Joan Kahn book."
   I. Title.
PR6063.A249L5   1984   823'.914   83-24657
ISBN 0-312-48387-2

First Edition

10 9 8 7 6 5 4 3 2 1

To Janette Holt

The
Life
and Death of
Liam Faulds

1

When he talked about his craft, Graeme Baldwin liked to say that he and other important novelists were holding a dialogue with their own subconscious minds while allowing the rest of humanity the privilege of eavesdropping on their private thoughts. Of course, he qualified this by adding that writers also had to have something vital and original to communicate and a style to match their ideas. However, as he glanced at the five authors round the lunch table, he wondered first why he was wasting time in such dubious company, then how they had ever bamboozled publishers into printing the trash they spawned and, finally, why the public bought and read the trash in such quantities. Every September, Baldwin and his fellow authors convened at a Park Lane hotel to award the Eddystone Prize of £5,000 for an Anglo-American novel that promoted good transatlantic relations, good English literature, or the art of the novel. Baldwin had earned his jury seat as a past winner. Yet, in his view, the Eddystone had become like most of these prizes—a literary charade monopolized by a handful of influential publishers to stimulate the sales of the half-dozen books on the short list, including the prize-winner. So profoundly did he detest the pretentious rite, he would have resigned long ago as a juror had his own publisher not twisted his arm by insisting that his appearance lifted his reputation and the sales of his own books. And he had to admit the Eddystone Prize had thrust his second novel into the best-seller bracket over twenty years ago, releasing him from hack writing and daily journalism. He did not take his jury service very seriously. Of the hundreds of books he received to consider for the short list, he read only those mentioned favourably by literary critics; as for the others, he looked at the jacket blurb, skimmed a few pages, and tossed them back with a *No*, stifling both his hypocrisy and his guilt complex. Nevertheless, Baldwin prided himself on being able to assess any author merely by reading and analyzing the style and construction of two or three paragraphs and observing how he handled a bit of narrative and a couple of scenes.

Waiters brought in the main course and served the six authors, the secretary of the Anglo-American Literary Circle who handled the Eddystone Prize administration, and the representative of the Eddystone Foundation, a trust established by a multinational electronics firm to finance education and cultural activities—and create prestige and publicity for the company. Before the silver helmets came off the trolleys, Baldwin smelled the roast lamb. Like the literary fare, you could tell the year by the menu, he reflected. Roast beef last year, roast lamb this year, roast veal next year, roast pheasant the year after, all irrigated with a throat-rasping Beaujolais. And the cycle recommenced.

Why did some sadist always sit him opposite Ronald Cranmore, a wizened homunculus with hooded eyes, a lizard face and buzzard neck? He wrote historical novels and had drunk so much British Museum book and parchment dust he had to chew charcoal biscuits continually for his ulcer, which gave him a tongue as black as a chow's and a chin dribbling with treacly saliva. He edited the literary magazine *Scroll*. Beside Cranmore towered Rosemary Grant Wayman, a big-bosomed Amazon with snow-white hair enclosing her skull like a bandanna, bristle on her upper lip and chin and a foghorn voice. American, she had written a dozen romantic novels set in Virginia during the War of Independence shot through with repressed sex. Another American, John Julian Rosen, a Bronx Jew, went in for blockbusting, documentary novels about the Great Society, dissecting big business and its tycoons and assembling thinly fudged portraits that grazed the defamation laws. America worshipped the deities of Eros and Mammon, which Rosen sublimated into explicit sex, crude violence and the pursuit of money by any means. He had made a fortune. Baldwin sat between him and the other English writer, Robert Gartland, who wrote animal sagas and ate most of his lunches in Regents Park zoo; he suffered from the English obsession for endowing animals with human feelings, articulate intelligence and an immortal soul, and failed to realize (according to Baldwin) that he and his fellow primates lived in the real zoo.

At the table head sat the jury chairman, John Anthony Bates, who looked like and was a fop, dressed in a velours hacking jacket and a silk shirt so frilly it resembled petrified champagne froth. A past winner of the Eddystone and reputed doyen of postwar English novelists, Bates had spent his literary lifetime piling up a cyclical novel in fifteen volumes depicting the fortunes of a middle-class family through two world wars that Baldwin found twice as long as its ten thousand pages, full of cut-out, middle-crust marionettes, and also written in lacklustre prose.

For this session they had short-listed the usual six books, though Baldwin considered only one merited any sort of distinction—Callum Laidlaw's *Lush Pastures*. He felt it could not miss the prize, and Bates agreed, whispering as they took their places that the book could hardly fail. Laidlaw had been one of Baldwin's best friends, and he had sponsored the book's posthumous appearance with a publishing house. Not his own, in case the jury and the press accused him of plugging one of his stable companions. They spooned through the invariable sorbet and were nibbling at the cheese board when Bates murmured in his Oxford drawl, "Well, lady and gentlemen, shall we pronounce on these?" He pulled the pile of books off the small side table as the waiters cleared away the dishes and brought in coffee. By now, everyone knew which books really stood a chance.

Bates, who had two votes but only used the second on split decisions, held up a small volume, *The Foundling*, a first novel by Jean Wakeford, a woman writer in her twenties. She had stood the usual adoption story on its head, recounting how a well-to-do young man who had lost his parents in an air crash and who was suffering from depression, had adopted an old couple ejected from their flat; gradually their love for him and their simple philosophy had pulled him out of his depression. When fire broke out in their building, the elderly husband sacrificed his own life to save the young man. Everyone praised Miss Wakeford's prose poem, the way she had handled the relationship of the trio and the emotion she had injected into the narrative. However, only one man voted for it: Baldwin. Seven pairs of eyes fixed on him, and the writers wondered if this was the usual Baldwin perversity. Few realized he had been a foundling himself and had identified with the orphaned youth.

Ronald Cranmore and Rosemary Wayman backed the first volume of a historical fresco by an American, Hogan Glendinning, eight hundred pages about the First Crusade with Jerusalem as its backcloth; it had the usual components, including unfettered sex, much blood-letting and star-crossed love between Christians and Saracens. "A splendid tome," Cranmore croaked, licking black lips.

"A small masterpiece," Rosemary Wayman intoned.

"Doesn't he just happen to publish with your American and British publishers?" Baldwin asked, wryly.

"That's got nothing to do with our judgement," Cranmore said.

"All right, but he's a has-been writer."

"A has-been! When he's only twenty-seven."

"I wasn't referring to his immaturity," Baldwin said. "He's an is-was writer. He uses every verb going providing they're ises and wases and has-beens." His comment was obviously orbiting over their heads. Stupid fools! Hadn't they read him and perceived how he manipulated English? Well, why should he divulge his literary discoveries? "Anyway, his book's so flat it would go under that door—both of them unopened," he muttered. Gartland concurred, Rosen abstained and Bates put in the clincher to reject the book.

Everyone contested Baldwin's vote on the third book, by a woman. In *The Eye of the Storm*, Janet Graystone had related the first-person story about an adolescent girl who fell in love with her father's younger brother, only to find he was also her mother's lover; she laid a sex trap for him and her mother that broke up the whole family and led, finally, to the girl's suicide. "A bit too Oedipus-complex by Freud out of Euripides and Aeschylus," Rosen commented.

"Myths are the axioms of the human soul," Baldwin retorted. He appealed, successfully, to the vestigial womanhood in Rosemary Wayman, who voted with him; but the others ganged together and defeated them. About the next book, *Run Wild, Run Free*, only Gartland had much good to report; however, as the autobiography of an African animal conservationist, it had hovered on best-seller lists for three months and hardly needed the Eddystone Prize boost.

Now came the bulkiest volume: *Overrun*. More than a thousand pastiche pages by Earl Grantham Mayne about the fight by a Kansas-Oklahoma border community to prevent the state and federal governments from invading prosperous farming land with a nuclear-power complex. Baldwin had spent no more than half an hour on this bloated tome. To him, it had every constituent of the phoney best-seller; pitched battles, a runaway reactor, murder, rape, arson, gratuitous violence. At least a dozen editors must have worked it over with Mayne, a mediocre writer; they had given it touches of *Gone With the Wind*, *Peyton Place*, *The Carpetbaggers*. It had everything except Indians and the soft-hearted gunfighter tussling with his no-smoking, no-drinking, no-killing and no-sex pledge. Baldwin knew its publisher had punted it into the American best-seller lists by purchasing several thousand copies in those shops where the press and TV channels took their book census. In biting terms, he condemned the book as flashy and trashy, unoriginal, unimaginative and unworthy of the Eddystone award. Gartland agreed, but Cranmore waxed eloquent about the book as did Rosemary Wayman. "Mayne gave the subject a highly intellectual flavour," she declared.

"Very intellechual," Baldwin sneered. "One of those intellechual Americans who think the James brothers were Frank and Jesse."

"Frank and Jesse?" Miss Wayman asked. "*I* know William and Henry James."

"Well, Mayne doesn't," Baldwin said with mordant sarcasm, drawing titters from Bates and Gartland.

Rosen intervened. "I thought the book had a lot of literary muscle," he said. In fact, several American states had banned the work for its frank and sometimes brutal portrayal of sexual behaviour.

"You're right about the muscle," Baldwin agreed, raising eyebrows all round. "But muscle surrounded by the gluteus maximus."

"Gluteus maximus?" Rosemary Wayman asked.

"He's talking about the human fundament, m'dear," Bates explained.

Baldwin looked at her. "What I really meant was the whole of this book's nothing like equal to the sum of its private parts."

Miss Wayman blushed to her beard roots and Bates swiftly diverted the argument by calling for a vote. Baldwin and Gartland voted against, Cranmore and Wayman for, and Rosen abstained. Everyone turned to Bates, who pushed the book aside, obviously undecided, and murmured that they might return to it. As the waiters chose this slight pause to replenish the coffee cups and liqueur glasses, Baldwin slipped out to the toilets.

"Whatever are we going to do about Baldwin?" Cranmore piped. "He's become a squalid, pernicious, insufferable boor."

"And he's a fine one to talk about has-been writers," Rosemary Wayman said. "They tell me his last three novels have sold fewer than five thousand copies in hardback and the paperback people aren't keen on them."

"And no film options," Cranmore added, his face crinkling in a dyspeptic smile. "They say Gresham and Holt have a warehouse full of *The Night Round* that they want to remainder but he won't let them because it would ruin his name."

"His latest effort, *A Savage Place*, is already doing that," Gartland whispered behind his hand.

"Now, now," Bates cautioned, raising an admonitory finger. "We mustn't be too hard on Baldwin. He's living on his nerves these days."

"On ours, you mean," Rosemary Wayman said.

"Why do writers get so schizo—?" Rosen was saying when Baldwin thrust open the door. He caught the last phrase, felt the hush and had the impression he had hosed them all with ice water or nerve gas; they sat like people petrified and he realized they had been playing that most ancient of literary games, denigrating living colleagues; he could almost smell their decayed comments hanging in the air like the pockets of Bates's stale cigarette smoke. He also sensed their personal enmity.

"Four down, one in the balance and one to go," Bates said, holding up *Lush Pastures*, the book by Callum Laidlaw that Baldwin had personally imposed on the Eddystone Prize jury. In his early journalistic days in Fleet Street he had worked with Laidlaw and therefore understood the man who had written this confessional novel, making himself its tortured anti-hero. A neurotic and misfit, Laidlaw had drunk himself to death at forty-five; for ten years he had toiled over this one book, which he never saw published but that Baldwin reckoned something of a masterpiece. As formless as a jumbled diary or a schizoid memoir, it was shot through with Laidlaw's sense of fear and guilt, his dread of both life and death. And since Laidlaw's conscious mind was swamped and numbed by liquor, every word had spilled with uninhibited candour from his subconscious mind, the purest type of autobiography. Some pages of that bitter poetry left Baldwin trembling; after reading the book he had walked round for days with Laidlaw's spectre at his side and those wounded phrases crawling through his brain like some obsessive tune.

Baldwin spent five minutes stating his defence of the book before Bates went round the table. Rosemary Wayman admired the writing but dismissed the work as prize material; Gartland had split thoughts; then Rosen spoke about the splendid reviews Laidlaw had received in America and gave it his vote. Now everything depended on Cranmore. Fixing Baldwin with his lizard eyes, he sneered and said, "I found this book a farrago of high-falutin' rubbish. Moreover, it's a bible for drunkards, a long hymn to alcohol."

"Ignoramuses who don't know a gin is also a trap say the same about *The Rubáiyát of Omar Khayyam*."

"Lush means a drunk," Rosen whispered to Rosemary Wayman, who seemed puzzled by the vehemence of the argument.

"Don't compare great literature to this gobbledygook," Cranmore cried through a fine charcoal mist.

Baldwin banged the table, rattling coffee cups and glasses. "I didn't expect somebody who writes pulp novels based on third-hand history to recognize either truth or talent when he meets it."

"Chairman, he's insulting me," Cranmore appealed to Bates.

"You insulted a friend of mine who can't answer back," Baldwin said. "Callum Laidlaw has written the purest personal truth out of his heart and mind. But how would somebody who camps half his life in the British Museum understand that?"

Bates called for order, then a show of hands on *Lush Pastures*. With a smirk (or a touch of wind?) Cranmore shook his head. Rosemary Wayman and Gartland kept their hands under the tablecloth. Bates looked at Baldwin, giving a shrug of resignation. Baldwin and Rosen dropped their hands, conceding defeat. Back came the thousand-page saga by Earl Grantham Mayne, for which Bates now voted before announcing that *Overrun* had won the Eddystone Prize.

At that, Baldwin drained his liqueur glass, muttered to the chairman that he had another appointment, nodded to the other jurors and marched out of the hotel. Dodging and slaloming between the Park Lane traffic he entered Hyde Park and stepped quickly westward, his feet keeping pace with the curses he was spitting at those impotent and spineless *litterateurs* who were back-scratching each other and voting at their publishers' dictates. Why had he trusted that grey-flannel man, Bates? Poor Callum Laidlaw's widow, who had nursed him through so many drunken crises, could have used that prize money and the extra royalties from his one book. To think that from hardback and paperback rights, film and TV contracts, book societies and foreign translations, Mayne would make more than a million dollars from that packaged and processed epic. Not even the autumn breeze trembling over the Round Pond cooled Baldwin's wrath.

Reaching Kensington High Street, he paused to deliberate if he should turn right for his own flat on Camden Hill, then finally decided he must go and break the bad news to Helen Laidlaw before she heard it on the radio. She lived in a top-floor flat at the seedy end of King's Road and Baldwin found a taxi to take him there. As he mounted the four flights of stairs, that odour of stewing beef and overboiled cabbage awoke memories of his orphanage boyhood. Helen met him at the flat door. A cigarette hung, inevitably, from her lips and gin perfumed her breath; but at least she was wearing a clean, hand-knitted cardigan and had evidently had her greying hair washed and set at a hairdresser's. She must have been expecting a descent in force by the press and TV. "Have you heard the bad news?" Baldwin asked.

"On the local radio," she wheezed in that Glasgow burr, thickened by a million cigarettes and as many gins.

"Sorry, Helen, I did my best," Baldwin murmured. "I know how much it meant to you."

"It wasna because o' the money, Graeme. He put so much into that book, did Callum."

"These prizes aren't worth a damn," he said. "Callum's book has truth in it and it'll be read when these phoney, fabricated best-sellers are dead and buried."

She conducted him into the small living room, where a youngish man rose and nodded at him. Helen introduced him as Martin Gilchrist, a first cousin of Callum's who free-lanced for his paper, the *Daily Globe*. Scanning the face under a blond thatch, noting the deep-set blue eyes and square chin, Baldwin knew he had met this man before, but he could not recall where. He explained to Helen how the voting had gone, how Bates had ratted on them and exactly what he thought of the other four jurors and the racket surrounding literary prizes generally. While he was speaking, Gilchrist produced a bottle of champagne, popped the cork with a bang and filled three glasses. "It was to drink to Callum and the prize," he said. "We can always drink to Callum." He was as Irish as whisky in coffee, Baldwin thought, noticing the flat Gaelic vowels and the twanging lilt of the Ulsterman, also how softly he spoke for such a big man. Baldwin was mentally evoking the faces he had encountered in Northern Ireland on his many trips there, but this one did not match any of them.

Helen Laidlaw appeared to sense his perplexity. "Martin helped with the serialization of *Lush Pastures* for the *Globe* colour supplement," she said.

10

"And I've the chance of putting together a radio serial based on the book," Gilchrist added.

They small-talked for twenty minutes until a spindly, fragile girl of about nine entered carrying a school satchel. Helen's only child. Baldwin seized his chance to escape. As he groped downstairs, heavy feet scuffed after him and Gilchrist caught him up on the outside steps. "You won't be remembering me, Mr. Baldwin, will you?" he asked.

"I'm sorry, I know we've met, but . . ."

"It was Belfast, at Queen's University. You came to give a talk about your books to the students' union and I was editing the university mag and I did a piece about you and your work."

"Of course!" Baldwin exclaimed. "We had several drams in the students' union." He smiled. "You did a good piece, too." In fact, Gilchrist had written a dithyrambic article that would have embarrassed him had the young student not sounded so sincere. He had even bought Gilchrist lunch at the Europa Hotel and could still remember the earnest face and halting confession of his new ambition—to become a good writer. It must have been what?—eight, nine years ago—not long after the start of the Northern Ireland troubles. "And now you're working on the *Sunday Globe*," he said.

"No, I freelance for several papers and magazines."

"Is there a living in that these days?"

"I keep my nose above water," Gilchrist replied. As they fell into step along King's Road, he mentioned he was married with a small daughter. He had refused a staff job in Fleet Street because he wanted to write seriously. In his view journalism tainted writers. Newsmen were always trailing after the event, back-tracking to salvage the bits and pieces of the revolution, the big crime, the accident or whatever, and this shaped their style, syntax and even their thought. Creative writers, on the other hand, fashioned their own world and their own literary form to describe it.

11

Baldwin listened to this discourse, blurted out with breathless conviction in that plangent Belfast voice. "Have you had anything published apart from your newspaper work?" he asked finally.

"No," Gilchrist admitted, sadly. "I start a novel or a play and halfway through I get bogged down . . . then I lose heart and start something else. I've done some short stories about Northern Ireland but there's no market for them, nowadays." He glanced at Baldwin, shaking his head in resignation. "If I only had a bit of your talent . . ."

Any minute now, Baldwin reflected, he'll ask me for my little secrets and how I use them; if I write with a goose quill or dictate into a tape machine; if I'm a nine-to-five man or wait for the muses or the divine flatus to move me. To deflect this line of talk he asked, "What are you doing about Callum and Helen?"

"I was supposed to do a piece on the prize, but that's kyboshed now," Gilchrist replied. "But listening to what you were saying just now about literary prizes and juries, I thought I might get away with a long feature article about the way they're rigged by publishing houses and their tame authors."

"You can quote me on that if you like."

"Now that would make a great piece," Gilchrist cried, so loudly that several people turned to stare at him. In a more subdued voice, he said, "Wouldn't that come back on you? I mean, wouldn't it be the end of you as a member of the Eddystone Prize jury?"

"They'll kick me out sooner or later," Baldwin said. He pointed to a café in King's Road. "Come on, I'll buy you a coffee and tell you how the racket operates and give you a few inside stories about the jurors, myself included, and I'll even put in a word with Jack Gibbon, the *Sunday Herald* editor, when you've written it." When they had found a table and ordered coffee, Gilchrist suddenly excused himself and left the café; five minutes later he returned holding up a new copy of *A Savage Place*, which he opened at the flyleaf for Baldwin to autograph.

"Why did you do that?" Baldwin muttered as he signed the book. "I'd have given you one of my free ones."

"I think it's a great book," Gilchrist said. "Helen lent me her copy."

"I wish even a few thousand more people agreed with your judgement."

"The public will catch up with you again in a year or two," Gilchrist declared.

Over coffee, Baldwin outlined how many of the literary juries operated, how publishers exercised subtle pressures on the jurors whose books they published to choose books from their own list for the prizes. His face incredulous, Gilchrist listened to the account of how books were coming to be marketed like toothpaste or dog meat and how the multinational firms were taking over publishing companies and running them like factories, how sales managers scrambled for a few minutes on radio or TV and even bribed critics and programme-makers—anything to get books into the top-selling bracket. What chance did budding authors have when publishers spent their money promoting only their big names and, if new books did not run away, they and their authors were dropped? Baldwin pitied the newcomers who had small chance of being published, let alone breaking through in competition with several hundred well-known authors.

"I can see I might as well give up trying," Gilchrist lamented, gulping his coffee and scribbling Baldwin's comments in a notebook.

"If you're hooked on writing you'll never do that," Baldwin said. "And if you do happen to get there, it's the nearest thing to being a free man. No unions, no big corporations, no constraints about where and how to live. Nobody to tell you what to write."

"That's my dream," Gilchrist whispered. He glanced over his notes—an amalgam of shorthand and scribble. "It's pretty explosive stuff you've given me," he remarked. "Do you want to have a look at the finished article in case you want to sub-edit some of it out?"

Baldwin shook his head. "I think I can trust you not to misquote me, and I meant every word I said."

They parted company outside the café. Baldwin hailed a cab to take him to Camden Hill. Heading homewards, he wondered idly what sort of fiction a naïve character like Gilchrist wrote.

2

A few days later, Baldwin let himself into his flat to find his daughter, Harriet, there. She put down her gassy fruit juice and crossed the living room to ricochet her cheek off his in a ritual greeting. Her presence meant she was cleaned out; both she and her mother had run through the allowance he made them. As he went to the drinks cabinet to slosh whisky into a glass, dilute it with water and a couple of ice cubes, he cursed under his breath at people who parasited on him—ex-wives, agents, tax men, publishers. He glanced, sourly, at the note his cleaner, Mrs. Taylor, had left on the table listing her shopping and cleaning expenses. She lived downstairs with her husband and on occasions cooked for him. Baldwin owned the whole house with its four flats (and its mortgage); he gave the Taylors the basement rent free for their services, rented the two upper floors and retained the ground floor and walled garden.

Harriet refilled her glass. Like her mother she was petite, blond and pert. "Mayne got the Eddystone Prize," she remarked.

"So they told me."

"It was good, *Overrun*. I enjoyed it."

"Crap it was, crap it is and forever will be."

"When you talk about anybody else's best-seller a green glow comes into your eyes," Harriet said, accusingly.

"In this case it's nausea, not jealousy," Baldwin countered. "I don't go in for literary competitions any longer."

"Maybe a good thing, since your last book wouldn't have had a chance," his daughter said. "You know Cecilia Parkstone ripped it to shreds in the *Sunday Herald*," she went on, naming a literary grande dame noted for her critical acerbity and her fine art of denigration.

"That old bitch," Baldwin spluttered through a spray of whisky. "Every author has acted as a scratching post for that old cat at some time or another."

"Mummy didn't like *A Savage Place*."

"Ah! now we're getting warm. I thought she only read the sales figures to estimate her next alimony cheque." For Baldwin, alimony had become an open wound; keeping his ex-wife and their daughter split his income almost in half.

"That's unfair," Harriet cried. "I can see why you couldn't live with anybody—you couldn't bear anybody disagreeing with you, the great author."

"I didn't mind when we were arguing and she was chucking things at me. It was when we stopped arguing and she got tired of throwing that life became too boring for us."

"You know when we watched *Stalemate* on television, Mummy said it was just like that between you from the very start."

"A bit like that," Baldwin conceded. A TV film had been made of one of his plays—a running battle between a young husband and wife about social position, money and sex that owed much to his own wrecked marriage. "What did she think of the film?"

Harriet shrugged. "She wasn't all that interested since she said she'd already played the lead in real life. She was more interested in your latest, the candy-floss blonde you

16

took along to the party before the film. Mummy didn't think she was all that pretty."

"Tell her they're more grateful that way."

Baldwin observed his daughter's grey-green eyes spark, like Diana's before she flexed her pitching arm. Mother and daughter resembled each other both in looks and character; they had the same casual irreverence, the same self-assurance and haughty manner. How much of himself had gone into the creation of this girl? Every time he studied her, it puzzled him. She had brittle, upper-crust features like some Nordic madonna; she had Diana's golden hair and straight nose, the same set of eyes, an ominous bit too close together, perhaps. Vainly he looked for a small contour from his angular face or Semitic nose (Arab or Jew, he didn't know which), a fleck from his brown eyes, even a crinkle from his curly brown hair. But Harriet seemed to have spurned every contribution he had made; all his mongrel chromosomes and myriad army of genes had somehow got sidetracked, swamped or shrivelled in contact with Diana's more vital reproductive cells. Yet he felt positive Harriet was his child, if only because of her perversity.

"I suppose I should have mentioned it, but Simon, my current boyfriend, is picking me up here," Harriet said. "He's a solicitor."

"What does all that mean—I have to feed him?"

"I can do the cooking if there's something in the fridge."

"Has this Simon ever sampled your cooking?" She shook her head. "Well, if you want to go on seeing him, either let me do the cooking or take him to the Church Street restaurant. I'll give you the money."

"Simon's got too much dignity to allow any girl to buy him a meal."

"He'll get over it." Baldwin went to the kitchen fridge and saw Mrs. Taylor had left a fillet steak, two pork chops, potatoes and broccoli. In the deep freeze, he identified four frankfurters. "We'll have to open a tin."

17

"Simon has a very delicate stomach."

"Then here's what we do. I suggest taking you both to the restaurant and at the last minute, Harry Seaborne rings me with urgent business and I send you both ahead. And Simon's face is saved." He pulled twenty pounds from his wallet. "Give this to André, the head waiter, and if Simon's too boozy or gourmand, I'll settle later with the restaurant."

Ten minutes later Harriet ushered in Simon and presented him. He had papyrus skin, receding hair and a beaky nose, and looked thirty-five. What was Harriet seeking? A life-insurance policy like her mother? He remembered when Diana and he had parted she had hit on a new philosophy: the happiest people lived ordinary, average lives up to the eyeballs in conformity, but of course with no money worries. Marginals like Baldwin only sowed strife and unhappiness. Well, nobody could be more ordinary than Simon Lutyens. Anybody who could talk so eloquently about conveyancing and make poetry out of land registry and last wills and testaments within five minutes of shaking hands obviously had a genius for normal life. Trembling with relief at his departure, Baldwin built himself two drinks in one and settled down to read the evening paper.

Yet, he could not concentrate. That joust with his daughter troubled him. How often recently had he heard that sort of value judgement on his work! Only a couple of days ago he had lunched with Harry Seaborne, his literary agent, and Keith Dunning, editorial director of Gresham and Holt, who had published the last thirteen of his books. Dunning reminded him of Simon—the same desiccated, sleet-gray face, the same spent small-talk. Dunning watered his wine and smoked cigarlets, afraid cigarettes would kipper his lungs with cancer. An Oxford drawl that had come with his Eng-Lit degree overlaid his blunter, more honest Yorkshire tongue. "It's a rotten period for sales, Graeme," he had said, muttering through pinched lips about the recession and linking this with the pile of unsold copies of Baldwin's *A Savage Place.*

18

"Best-sellers are still selling," Baldwin remarked.

"Nothing much else, though," Harry Seaborne put in. "It's a bad year, Graeme. A sunspot year."

Dunning had balanced a sugar cube on a spoon, submerged it in his coffee and sucked it; he'd turned tired eyes on Baldwin, their blue bleached from scanning billions of words that the writer reckoned never penetrated beyond the retina of Dunning's eyes. "Got to look at the hard-tack, Graeme," he said. "Your last three books haven't exactly set Old Father Thames ablaze, have they now?" He sucked another cube. "You've read your royalty statements."

"I'm writing as well as I've ever done."

"Yes, but maybe you need a fresh slant on things," Seaborne put in again, and Baldwin had glowered at him. Some authors' agents worked honestly for their writers, others threw in their lot with publishers and damned their authors, and people like Seaborne played both sides off against the other.

"You need a rest," Dunning said. "Why don't you have a sabbatical, lock up your machine and take off into the blue for at least a year?"

"Keith's right," Seaborne said. "You've done a book a year for over fifteen years, Graeme, sometimes two. Let them wait a bit for the next one. Scarcity value—cultivate scarcity value."

Baldwin had listened to enough of Dunning's strictures and Seaborne's slogans; he'd gulped down his coffee and, without saying a word, walked out of the restaurant, leaving them to their inquest on his work. "To hell with Dunning," he muttered to himself. "If I sent him a book written on shithouse paper by an illiterate, spastic, six-fingered Swahili in pidgin English, he'd rave about it and give it the big publicity build-up. Or if I did him a New Wave novel copied from some Left Bank, French-fried frog writer with no beginning, no end and very little middle and a load of metaphysical pap, he'd extol its genius and sell all of twelve copies." They could both talk. Neither of them had to pay hefty alimony and struggle to meet his taxes. One had his director's screw and the other a string of authors sweating their brains out for him. If a couple of novels went down, he, Baldwin, would find himself on his uppers and they wouldn't give a damn since they'd be battening on the latest literary champion. To hell with publishers and lackey agents!

Maybe he shouldn't have phoned Elaine that afternoon but waited until his temper had cooled. Elaine was his mistress and worked as a copy writer in an advertising agency. Baldwin needed somebody to be with, to talk to; he had gone to her flat and she had made him a meal. But somehow, as they were eating, she mentioned a critic who had slated *A Savage Place* and they began to argue about it, then quarrel and finally Baldwin threw down his napkin and stalked out on her. What the hell did he need with any of them!

Baldwin wrenched his concentration back to the evening paper and suddenly his eye lighted on the long horse face of John Huston, the film director. In an hour's time on TV they were showing one of his classic films, *The Treasure of the Sierra Madre*. Normally, Baldwin never looked at television beyond the nine o'clock news, but tonight the thought of working or serious reading repelled him. He would watch the Huston film, then bed early, he decided. In the kitchen, he thawed out a couple of frankfurters, grilled them and heated some tinned spinach to go with them. This he ate on a table in front of the TV set, washing it down with a can of lager and finishing with cheese, biscuits and coffee as he watched the film. Its story was simple. Two young Americans and a veteran decide to hunt for gold in the hills of northern Mexico. Despite great hardship and opposition from Mexican Indians they discover a rich seam and mine it. While the old man (played by Walter Huston, the director's father) goes off to treat sickness among an Indian tribe, the two others quarrel over their treasure; Dobbs (Humphrey Bogart) kills his partner and makes off with the gold on mules. However, he is caught and killed by the Indians, who

20

look on with indifferent eyes at the gold dust scattering in the wind. Baldwin was seeing the film for the first time though he had read the book years ago, viewing it as a morality tale about gold lust and greed and capitalist villainy meeting their desserts from innocent savages.

He had completely forgotten about the author, one of the great mystery men of modern literature. After the film they did a portrait of this strange being who called himself B. Traven. Baldwin watched, enthralled. He had to hand it to Traven, who had fooled and eluded everybody by inventing half a dozen aliases and having another dozen pinned on him by journalists who had lost his trail. Whole teams of reporters and writers had spent half a century trying to solve the mystery and pierce Traven's real identity. Some thought him a Norwegian named Berick Traven Torsvan (the name on his Mexican passport), while others claimed he was a renegade American, Hal Croves (another of his aliases), who had fled to Mexico to escape the FBI. Still others pushed the story further, believing him to be a German communist propagandist called Ret Marut who had been chased by Hitler in the thirties and feared for his life so much that when he landed in Mexico he concealed his real identity under several cover names. In turn, Ret Marut (some imagined him a bastard son of Kaiser Wilhelm II) was probably a *nom de plume* for a young German political activist called Hermann Feige. Hardier journalists even suggested the name Traven camouflaged an American writer who had disappeared in mysterious circumstances, like Ambrose Bierce, or one who had clearly died, like Jack London.

Baldwin turned off the set and went to warm his cold coffee. He could not switch his mind away from the image of that gaunt-faced will-o'-the-wisp figure reputed to be Traven. With his phoney Mexican passport and a few accommodation addresses he had given everyone the slip, and kept on deceiving them beyond his grave. Moreover, his fetish for anonymity had set the whole world running after him—and devouring his books by the ton. Civilized man detested unsolved riddles; so

Traven's self-made legend boosted his books, lending them another dimension. To Baldwin he acted like a man on the lam who, despite himself, was stumbling and backing into the limelight. Baldwin burned his fingers with the match he had already applied to the gas. His mind ranged elsewhere: Would Traven's books, like *The Death Ship* and *Sierra Madre*, have made anything of an impact if their author had dropped his umpteen masks? Baldwin considered them lightweight—just good, first-hand portraits of stokers and ships' crews, of down-and-outs and miners-on-the-make with a leavening of socialist morality and a naïve yen for primitive freedom *à la Rousseau*. When he reflected, Baldwin realized Traven didn't hold the patent on literary puzzles. The eternal who-wrote-Shakespeare argument helped to keep the plays alive. And who wrote Ossian—a third-century Gaelic bard, or an eighteenth-century Scot called Macpherson? Did Homer, the so-called blind poet, exist, let alone put the *Iliad* and *Odyssey* together? Even Walter Scott gained notoriety from acting as the Great Unknown author of *Waverley* and other novels. Would Jack the Ripper have made so much criminal and literary stir had he been caught? And the *Marie Celeste*? Who would remember that phantom ship if one single witness had remained alive to tell the tale?

3

A thought struck Baldwin with such force that it dumped him in a chair at the kitchen table and plunged him into a trance of reflection. Perhaps he needed the Traven touch! As a creative writer why shouldn't he imagine a completely new identity for himself, change his style and thrust out in an entirely fresh direction? He let the coffee foam over the saucepan rim, dousing the flame under it until the cloying odour of gas pulled him out of his reverie. He turned off the gas and carried the coffee through the living room into his small study. He sat there for long minutes, sipping the bitter liquid and staring into the dusk-filled garden, its lawn barbered to perfection by old Taylor, its roses glowing like candles and Bengal matches, its phloxes and delphiniums disposed geometrically in neat phalanxes. A bit of mystery. Maybe that's what he required to set him going again. Dunning was amortizing him as a man on the slide and the lickspittle Seaborne, whom he had kept for twelve years with his ten percent, was getting ready to desert. Trouble was, they had something. His cuttings book, with reviews of his three latest novels and personal press comment, had grown nowhere near as fat as the previous half-dozen, and critics now spiked their brief notices with sarcasm and scorn. However, in his den, he could still draw comfort from a whole wall of his books in twenty different tongues, the first-night pictures of his three plays and his own portrait gallery with a dozen international celebrities. Damn it, he was writing as well now as when he'd won the Eddystone Prize over twenty years ago. Only the public appeared to have grown blasé with their yearly "Baldwin" for the beach, the chalet or cruise liner.

How he'd love to produce a best-seller and ram it, page by page, down the gullets of Dunning and Seaborne! Preferably published by another firm to light a fire under Dunning's stomach ulcer every time he spotted the display in booksellers' windows; he could even let another agent handle the book and watch the rapacious Seaborne squirm. At the same time, he'd love to score at least one point off his ex-wife and dock her allowance. That layabout architect she was shacked up with would have to go out to work if her alimony dried up. Still another buzzard squatted over his bank account—the tax man. Over the years they'd soaked him enough. For what? To buy a pinch of plutonium for another nuclear warhead, or a jump-jet engine or some other defence toy. Bloodsuckers the lot of them. If only he could spike all their guns. . . .

He shifted his gaze to the bookcase over his writing table, to the manuscript he had almost finished. Revised and polished, it would normally go to Dunning within a month, to appear in nine months' time for the holiday trade. What neither Dunning nor Seaborne nor anybody else knew was that he had another manuscript, written piecemeal over the last two years and placed on his shelf. Like many writers, Baldwin had a whole bagful of phobias about drying up or hitting a bad patch; so he kept a script in reserve against that day. Now, he took the two typescripts and leafed through the finished one, entitled *A Place to Die*. It told the story of two self-seeking middle-class people who had chosen their careers before their marriage. He was a high-ranking civil servant aiming for a knighthood and she was a barrister who wanted to become a judge. Finally, they divorced and their twelve-year-old son oscillated between them, more at home with their servants than with them. When the boy fell ill and leukaemia was diagnosed, the mother moved back with the father to help nurse him, though neither sacrificed his or her career. When the boy escaped from the sick room to seek out their retired housekeeper and die in her small bed-sitting room, both parents realized they had failed him; yet, at the graveside, they swallowed their remorse, stiffened their upper lips and went their separate careerist ways. Baldwin read a few pages of that manuscript before replacing it on the shelf. Timeless stuff which he could release when he felt like it.

He opened the second manuscript, which still lacked a final chapter. Within minutes it had engrossed him with its Northern Ireland background of fratricidal violence, religious fanaticism and star-crossed love. During the height of the riots, killings and bombings in Ulster, the *Sunday Herald* had commissioned him to write a series of articles. He had spent four months in Belfast and Londonderry as well as provincial towns, meeting people of all classes and recounting their plight. On this trip he had met Martin Gilchrist. One story had touched him so deeply he'd felt it would work only as fiction; as a factual account, no one would have believed it and he could never have given it the same scope or depth of feeling. Even then he had incubated the story for eight years, hesitating to relate it in novel form in case the critics would accuse him of cribbing Shakespeare's *Romeo and Juliet*, merely substituting two Catholic and Protestant families for the warring Montagues and Capulets. But he had actually met the Catholic O'Donnells, who lived in Divis Street, right in the battleground between the sects, and the Montgomerys, well-to-do Protestants from the residential district the other side of the Lagan River. Seamus O'Donnell, head of the house, had joined the Irish Republican Army in the thirties and had taken part in the bombing campaign for Irish unity in Britain shortly before the Second World War. His two sons, Fergal and Peadar, had become hard-line members of the Provisional IRA, but his daughter, Kathleen, refused to associate herself with the IRA or sectarian violence. On the Protestant side, David Montgomery, a leading member of the Ulster Defense Association, had three sons. Tom, the eldest, was a solicitor and a reserve policeman in the Royal Ulster Constabulary; Brian, another militant Protestant, worked as a design draughtsman in the Harland and Wolff shipyards; Hugh, the youngest, was studying medicine at Queen's University and would have no part in religious or social strife. Both Seamus O'Donnell and David Montgomery symbolized the violent intransigence of their movements; both had committed armed raids and bombings and O'Donnell, who had been caught, had served two years in jail. They detested each other.

Kathleen O'Donnell was training to be a teacher; she had met Hugh Montgomery at a lunchtime chamber-music concert in the university. Without asking whether they were Catholic or Protestant, long before they discovered anything about each other's family, they fell in love. When they did find out more about each other, they decided to ignore sectarian politics and their family feud. However, they kept their love to themselves and met clandestinely outside the Northern Ireland capital.

In her home one night, Kathleen overheard an IRA plot to plant a car bomb in the Crumlin Road area and then ambush the policemen from the local jail when they came to investigate the blast. She realized Hugh's brother Tom was doing duty that night at the station and ran to warn him about the ambush. A constabulary detachment set a trap for the IRA gang. Opening fire on the stolen car, they detonated the gelignite in it and blew up the two men inside. Peadar O'Donnell, Kathleen's brother, died in that explosion. Four other IRA men were killed in the gun battle that started afterwards. Before Peadar O'Donnell was buried, the Provisional IRA command ordered an inquiry into the treachery. Suspicion fell on the O'Donnells and the girl had to confess. Not even her father's status prevented the court-martial from sentencing her to head-shaving and knee-capping (shooting through the knee) as a punishment. Kathleen did not wait for them to carry out the sentence; she fled across the city to Hugh Montgomery, who hid her with one of his aunts. Knowing that the IRA vengeance squads would never rest until they had executed the sentence, Hugh and Kathleen made plans. They would head for London where they would get married and he would finish his medical training; they'd seek an out-of-the-way practice and, to make sure nobody would find them, they'd change their names. Their plans came to nothing. Someone, probably a militant Protestant, gave Kathleen away and an IRA murder gang besieged her hideout flat. Alerted by phone, Hugh and Tom arrived and tried to fight off the gunmen. Hugh was killed and Tom seriously wounded before an RUC patrol scattered the IRA men. Seamus O'Donnell brought Kathleen home. He vowed to quit the IRA and take half a dozen important families with him if they laid a finger on his daughter. This time the IRA desisted, having exacted its revenge by killing Hugh.

Six months later, Kathleen's body was recovered from the Lagan just below Queen Elizabeth Bridge. In a short note, she begged her Catholic family's pardon for the mortal sin of suicide and pleaded to be buried with Hugh Montgomery, her only love. Since he worshipped his daughter, Seamus O'Donnell had to pocket his pride and beseech David Montgomery for permission to honour his daughter's last wish. Not only did Montgomery agree but he arrived with his two sons at the graveside to join O'Donnell and his surviving son in prayers for the dead couple. There was no service. Catholic priests refused to bury Kathleen, a suicide and a traitor to the Irish cause, and no Protestant pastor would have dared to hold a graveside service for a Catholic with IRA connections.

Baldwin skimmed through the manuscript, halting here

and there to read certain scenes. He didn't much like his provisional title, *The Heart Knows No Treason*, but he would hit on something with more bite. Without real awareness of why he did it, he ran a thick, red pencil through his own name on the title page and wrote in "by Liam Faulds." Although the name had flashed, unbidden, into his mind, it sounded right. How would a publisher react on receiving this novel by an unknown Irish author? Why shouldn't he try submitting it and watch what happened? The more he considered the idea, the more it appealed.

What a kick in the brisket for Dunning and Seaborne if this novel reached the best-seller lists under a different name! Or won something like the Eddystone Prize! Except that nobody was allowed to win the Eddystone Prize twice. When they pierced his alias, they'd chuck the book out. Baldwin knew the tale-telling, tongue-wagging publishing world too well to imagine his pseudonym would keep them guessing long. If he used that name, Liam Faulds, he must make it absolutely fireproof. B. Traven was a lucky man since nobody knew him or could identify him. Baldwin had no such advantage, having appeared all over the media. Thus, he would need not only a *nom de guerre* but several baffle walls between him and publishers, critics, journalists and the authorities. What he required was a decoy, somebody to represent the mysterious real author of *The Heart Knows No Treason*. No reason why he shouldn't work out an agreement with the person playing his decoy and pay him a bit more than the agent's ten percent for his trouble. Of course he'd have to rewrite the whole book, for every critic, British and American, would recognize his style in the present manuscript.

Baldwin sat watching darkness engulf his walled garden and fill his study. In his mind, he turned the problem over, holding it up like some raw diamond he was cutting and polishing until each facet glittered, brilliant and clear, and every flaw had vanished. He rang Dunning at home. "Keith, I've been thinking about our chat the other day," he said. "You're right, I need a long rest."

"Good man," Dunning said. "But before you take off, we'll have the book you've been working on, won't we?" Suddenly, he sounded apprehensive, as though suspecting a trick or defection to another publisher.

"Sorry, not yet," Baldwin replied. "I've had another shufti at it and it looks as if I'll have to rip it to bits and cobble it together again. As it reads now, it's not worth printing."

"We'd still like to have a look at it, ol' boy."

"You shall—if and when I'm ready," Baldwin murmured, enigmatically, and hung up. Ringing Seaborne with the same message, he noted with satisfaction the disquiet in his agent's voice.

He rang Helen Laidlaw for Gilchrist's number and address, then cross-examined her discreetly about him and his background. She had not met his wife, but could not praise Gilchrist too highly. "He was the most loyal friend we had when Callum was taken bad," she said. "I'd trust him with my life."

Gilchrist answered the phone himself, and Baldwin asked if he had written and filed the article about the literary prize racket. Gilchrist replied that he had done all the research and was just putting the story together.

"Well, do me a big favor and cut out all my quotes and any mention of my name," Baldwin said. "But of course you can use the information I gave you without attributing it to anybody."

Gilchrist raised no objection, merely suggesting he would like to meet Baldwin again; he had those short stories he wanted to show him. Baldwin seized on this cue to invite the Irishman over for a drink in two weeks' time. After he replaced the phone, he picked up the Ulster manuscript again. While listening to Gilchrist's Belfast accent he had suddenly realized what this book demanded—somebody like

29

Gilchrist to tell the story in his own speech, somebody, say, like the girl's surviving brother who had chosen a cover name, Liam Faulds. What if the narrator belonged to the IRA and had perhaps taken part in several criminal actions and was wanted by the police? Wouldn't that make the tale so much more poignant? It would also explain all the complicated precautions the author had adopted to avoid divulging his true identity. For Baldwin it threw up composition and construction problems; he would have less freedom of manoeuvre to relate the love story; on the other hand, he could take any liberties he liked with style since he was using the speech and vocabulary of an average Irishman. So far, he had written every one of his books in the third person; a first-person story would therefore divert suspicion away from him.

Baldwin brewed himself another couple of pots of coffee and settled down for a long session. First, he rapped out the scheme of the book as it stood, then dismembered the manuscript and rearranged the pages into those that would stand alone without rewriting and those he could discard; after this, he began the complex task of scheming the construction of the new book, seen through another person's eyes. He would have to write several new chapters and deepen the relationship between Kathleen O'Donnell and her brother, Fergal, who was recounting her story. If this constricted the physical scope of the novel it lent much more poignancy and pathos to the final scene at the graveside. As an IRA man wanted for a dozen offences, the brother did not dare appear but viewed the scene through field glasses from a hideout flat.

Even with his acute ear for dialogue, Baldwin struggled to imagine the style and speech patterns of an Ulster Catholic and to get inside the skin of a terrorist gunman. To help him, he went back to his own notes and articles written during his Ulster assignments. Strangely, after he had composed the first four pages, he started to see and sense his own narrative through an Irishman's eyes and hear some of the dialogue in that Irish-Scots vernacular with its Gaelic twists. More curious still, he began to conceive the story in the Belfast twang and the sort of phrases Gilchrist used. As the night wore on, he identified himself so thoroughly with the characters he had already invented, and those he added, that present time and place hardly mattered. Only when daylight crept over the page and swamped the glow of the reading lamp did he realize he had been toiling for fully nine hours. He got up, shaky with fatigue, wedged himself into the study armchair and fell fast asleep.

When Ina Taylor arrived later that morning to clean the flat, she came on him, still snoring with his head arched back against the chair. All round him, littering the desk and floor, lay a whole book like some wild leaflet raid; annotations in red and green ink covered the margins and strips of paper with additions in Baldwin's scrawled handwriting were stuck to the original manuscript pages. Mrs. Taylor knew better than touch them; she shrugged and tut-tutted, recognizing the syndrome. He called it going into purdah. Sometimes these frenzied writing bouts lasted a week, sometimes a month or two. With her fingertips she nudged him and he woke with a startled throw of his head, then stared at her like some intruder before he realized he was in his own study and not in the Falls Road or Divis Flats or where the Montgomerys lived across the Lagan. He mumbled an apology for the mess, then issued the usual orders. His fridge and drinks cabinet needed stocking for at least a fortnight. She would take in the milk and papers. If anyone called at the house he would not answer the door; if they approached her she would lie in her teeth that he had gone away for an indefinite period. He would take his phone out of commission. She could come into the flat for an hour a day to clean the kitchen and living room; she must not touch the study.

With Mrs. Taylor gone, he brewed himself another lot of coffee, fried himself two eggs, which he ate, followed by toast and marmalade, at his study desk. Until he had broken the back of the new script, he would remain here, alienated from everything and everyone that might distract him from living with his characters in their environment. He would live and breathe them until they had taken full shape on the page; any revision or refining he could do later, at his leisure. Baldwin had his own strict rules. While working on the magma of a book he behaved like a boxer or an athlete in training; he would neither listen to the radio nor look at TV, though he might play the odd piece of classical music or jazz on his record player; he read neither newspapers nor books and during the day he would even draw the curtains to shut out the disturbing view of his garden. All this he did in the interests of Realism, though well aware that chameleon words could never adequately express emotion or describe anything exactly. Which two people ever gave any word precisely the same significance? Baldwin had his writing fetishes; at the end of his working day, he would never complete the last thought he was developing but leave it hanging, even in mid-sentence, so that he had something to grasp and set him going the next day. Before putting out his light, he let each of his main characters flit through his brain with the part of the plot he was creating; in this way, he hoped ideas and thoughts would erupt out of his subconscious mind while he slept. At the start of each book, he drew rough portraits of the principal characters, or cut some likeness of them out of magazines. These pictures he pinned on the blank wall of his study with a thumbnail biography beside them. Maps, charts, and documents joined them on the wall, eventually lending the study the appearance of an operations room. He typed his thoughts straight onto paper, using only one-half of the page, reserving the other for corrections and additions that he often pasted over the original draft. Outlining each book occupied him for about a month; then he spent six or seven more months rewriting and revising two or three successive drafts. He never employed a secretary or a typist, letting nobody touch his work until it went to the publishers, and even they could not carry out alterations without consulting him. Finally, he locked away the typescript for at least two months when finished so that his mind would erase much of its detail and he could read it with a fresh eye.

For eighteen days, often extending far into the night, Baldwin toiled in complete isolation, dissecting the Irish novel and recasting it as a first-person story. At the end of that time, he had a hefty and lumpish typescript, stuck or stapled throughout with corrections and additions. Of the original book he had salvaged two-thirds and had interleaved another third with new material to bring on Kathleen O'Donnell's brother Fergal as narrator. It would require another couple of weeks to rework the eighty thousand words and retype the book. But this he could do any time.

He felt drained, voided, as he always did after finishing one of these writing marathons. Staggering round the flat, he parted the living-room and bedroom curtains and opened windows to admit fresh air, which only brought home how stale and malodorous the place had become with tobacco smoke and fried fat and his own presence and breath. Still in his shirt, pullover and trousers, he collapsed on the bed and stared at the ceiling, his mind reflecting its anonymity. Flaubert, Zola and their pals had got it right; literary creation sucked everything out of you, leaving nothing for sex or any other emotion, sapping even the energy for normal living. Baldwin drowsed on that thought, then plummetted into sleep. When he woke, the light was thickening in the corners and around the bedroom furniture. Peeling off his clothes, he stepped into the shower and for a quarter of an hour sluiced hot then cold water over his body. As he shaved off his ten-day beard, every razor stroke revealed more of his haggard face and collapsed cheeks and hollow eyes. For nearly three weeks he had switched off; now he experienced the urge to plug himself back into the life stream. He toyed with the notion of phoning Elaine, softening her up with sweet words, buying her a banquet at the Ritz and spending the night at her flat. But no, damn her, he couldn't dent his pride like that.

When he had dressed he poured himself three fingers of Scotch and sipped it, neat, before wandering down to Kensington High Street, where he pointed his cab towards Luigi's restaurant behind Charing Cross Road. Luigi, a flat-footed Neapolitan he had known as a waiter in one of Forte's eating houses, understood what he wanted—smoked salmon and a Pouilly, then a tournedos steak like a pair of boxing gloves, with a rich Romanée followed by a wedge of Roquefort, zabaglione and black coffee.

At eleven o'clock, watered and fed, he strolled through Leicester Square to Piccadilly and circled the Regent Palace Hotel. If any of the girls there remembered him they betrayed no sign, and that comforted him. He wasn't looking for intellectual companionship—just a common prostitute he could drag down to his own level of human vulgarity and animal passion for this night. She stood on the corner of Swallow Street, reddish-blond, thirtyish with a fringe over wide-spaced eyes, good breasts and a chirpy French intonation as she called, *"Bon soir, chéri."* He spoke only restaurant French and she little English so he could take cover behind the language barrier. She probably spent a hundred one-night stands a year in the Regent Palace, but acted as though she had been Madame Harry Seaborne for a decade to judge by the cool poise with which she handled the cynical hotel porter. Fifty pounds she demanded. And she earned it. Neither in the literature of erotica nor even in the best-scripted all-in wrestling matches had Baldwin ever met several of the positions they both achieved that night. To show his appreciation he left another ten pounds on the dressing table as he slipped out of the hotel before dawn to avoid meeting her when she woke. He did not even know her trade name. But any charm such women had for him dissolved in daylight. And they left him with an aftertaste of guilt about surrendering to the sort of lust that must have gone into his own making.

Back in his flat later that morning, he restored the phone line. His first call came from Martin Gilchrist. "I've been trying to get you for more than ten days," he said, apologetically. "I couldn't make it the night you invited me."

"My fault," Baldwin replied. "I should have rung to say I was going away."

"I came over to tell you, but the flat looked shut up and the woman downstairs said you'd been called away urgently on an assignment."

"I've just got back," Baldwin said, thinking that about summed things up. "Give me a few days to settle in and then drop by . . . no, let's say a bit longer, two weeks today . . . Friday. If you can, make it fairly early . . . ten o'clockish . . . and bring your stories for me to have a look at them." Gilchrist sounded delighted at the idea.

Baldwin went back into his study. During those two weeks he reworked the new script, then went out and photocopied the three hundred and twenty manuscript pages. He shopped for an up-to-date guide book, large-scale maps of Northern Ireland, street plans of Belfast, Derry, Enniskillen and other Ulster towns. He had a lot of work to do before meeting Gilchrist.

4

As a man without any real roots or even a real name, Baldwin realized he was running several risks by changing his literary identity. Writing was a solitary, introspective game and he knew so many authors who lived in uneasy symbiosis with their fictional creations, stepping in and out of their bodies and brains. Sometimes they even lapsed into a schizophrenic coexistence with their characters, and the paper figures they had fashioned actually seemed to take charge of both writer and story, transforming them. Now, he was not only constructing a new literary self but a "live" plot to go with it, and one on which his own future might depend. He must rule out every possibility of error: he would have to choose the right, real-life characters to play their parts in the plot alongside himself; he must erect several barriers between himself and his alter ego, Liam Faulds, so that he not only protected himself against exposure but safeguarded his own title to the Faulds book; but above all, to make this plot work he had to get inside this man, Liam Faulds.

Liam Faulds was not his only alias. For, although the name Graeme Baldwin was on his birth certificate, it meant no more to him than the pseudonym he had stuck on two of his novels. He had never known his parents and could not even believe his birth date on that official form. He was a bastard, unclaimed by both father and mother and deposited in his first fragile weeks on church steps near London Bridge. A devout cleaning woman, Margaret Baldwin, carried him to the nearest Everopen Home for orphans; she also gave him half his name and breastfed him for four months. His first name came from James Graham, warden of the boys' home where Baldwin spent all his childhood and part of his adolescence.

Those years shaped his life, toughened his nature and taught him the race was to the ruthless, the calculating, the cunning. He suffered torture from a gang of bully boys until the day he and another boy ambushed one member on his own and roughed him up so badly he spent three days in hospital. For that insolence, Baldwin was challenged by Jeff Grain, the gang leader, to a three-round boxing match, the ritual way of settling scores. Graham acted as referee. Baldwin realized he would never survive unless he acted, so he palmed two inches of lead pipe in his sparring gloves. For two rounds, he took a battering, but in the final round Grain grew cocky, leaving his face and head exposed. Baldwin scythed at it with his right hand and cracked Grain on the temple with the lead pipe. They carried him from the ring, senseless.

At twelve, Baldwin discovered somebody was thieving from his and other lockers. Complain to the warden and the other boys would have thrashed him stupid. So he spent his pocket money in a Lambeth pet shop acquiring a viper that he placed in his locker. Two days later, when most boys were playing or watching soccer, screams rent the main building. A senior prefect called Alex Laurence was running for the warden's office, terrified. Baldwin arrived as Graham was examining two bluish punctures on the boy's hand. He let the petrified Laurence imagine he had been bitten by a poisonous snake until he confessed to the pilfering.

Several couples wanted to adopt Baldwin, but something always wrecked the process; either he behaved badly or spurned his future guardians. When two people had nearly clinched his adoption, he saved himself by reaming off a string of four-letter oaths and insulting the woman. Visiting days terrified him since they might spell the end of his days at the orphanage. It was a long time before he realized he did not want to lose the Grahams. He had made James Graham, a New Zealander, his hero, and he had fallen in adolescent love with Graham's wife, Elizabeth. Who as beautiful, gentle and kind as she would claim him? He watched the faces of the other boys, crowding around the windows, observing couples drive their coveted cars into the courtyard, their young eyes filled with a longing to escape. They reminded him of those dogs in the lost-and-found compound at the Battersea dog home.

Ironically, the orphanage turned him into a writer. A loner, he spent hours wondering who had borne him only to abandon him. Where had those brown eyes come from? And what might pass for a Yiddish nose? And the long face and gangling body? He made up romantic tales, explaining his parents' betrayal and either excusing them or damning them to hell. Later, he realized that in these stories he was taking refuge from the harsh world in a universe of his own creations. His favourite corner was the Grahams' small library of second-hand and gift books near their lodge; there, Baldwin spent most of his leisure time devouring literature by the mile. He read every one of the hundreds of novels in the library and discovered the marvels in Shakespeare, Fielding, Smollett, Scott, Dickens, Thackeray, and the moderns like Bennett, Wells, D. H. Lawrence and Virginia Woolf; he read good translations of Flaubert's *Madame Bovary* and those powerful Zola novels of seamier life and cracked his head on Gide and Proust; he marvelled at the art and psychological insight of Dostoevsky and wondered at the mysticism and curious morality of Tolstoy, who looked and wrote like God Himself. All of these writers became milestones in his literary formation. Scenes from their books imprinted themselves on his mind like so much cinema. He had no pretensions of competing with the illustrious dead let alone the moderns, but he began to study the hundred-odd orphans, fitting each with a biography. In that London district, near the docks, the boys arrived in all shapes, sizes and colours; many had mixed blood with one Chinese, Indian or African parent and felt like pariahs outside the institution. Indeed, many had such complexes about race and colour they left the orphanage and landed in a borstal or in prison, having committed some stupid crime.

One story that Baldwin picked up fixed his own future. When he was fourteen he began to observe a wealthy, neurotic couple, the Flemings, who came to adopt a boy; they seemed never to stop quarrelling, even in Graham's company. Finally, they chose a boy that everybody else had spurned, a spindly, sickly youth of twelve called Hockley. Soon their reasons became clear; they wanted a whipping boy, someone on whom they could vent their neurotic tempers. Hockley stood many beatings before running away and reaching the Everopen Home; however, his official adoption had gone through and the Flemings persuaded Graham to give them another chance before attempting to annul the adoption. In a curious way, Hockley was holding their marriage together, as the son they could never have and as their safety valve. Yet, they treated him no better. Within a year he had escaped for good. Caught shop-lifting, he admitted some twenty-five other offences and finished in a borstal institution. No one showed more solicitude than the Flemings. They visited him twice a week and lobbied their MP and the Home Office to seek early release. If he forgave them and returned, they promised never to lay a finger on him. And this time they kept their word, for now they needed him to give their lives some point. Hockley exploited their weakness and by gentle threats and a little blackmail was soon running the whole household with the Flemings taking orders from him.

Baldwin showed his story, "The Whipping Boy," to his secret love, Elizabeth Graham. After she read it she looked at him and smiled. "But, Graeme, you're a writer," she murmured. He needed no other encouragement. Her husband knew the editor of a small magazine called *Meridian* and persuaded him to print the story. He paid Baldwin thirty shillings while remaining sceptical about a fourteen-year-old orphan boy who had such a profound knowledge of human behavior. That cheque, dated November 2, 1951, hung in a small frame above Baldwin's study mantelpiece reminding him not only of his first literature earnings but the fact that "The Whipping Boy" had saved him from some humdrum job or perhaps landing in prison like so many orphanage boys.

Before he left the home, *Meridian* printed two more stories and this enabled James Graham to persuade the local newspaper editor to hire Baldwin as a dog's body in his one-room editorial office. Soon, having mastered a bastard shorthand and two-fingered typing, Baldwin was covering everything from dog shows and jumble sales to the police courts and local council meetings; he wrote several stories, bought by various magazines, and a novel about orphanage life which a dozen publishing houses rejected and which he finally scrapped. At eighteen, he moved west and across the Thames to Fleet Street as a reporter, first for the Press Association, then, the *News Chronicle*.

Baldwin and newspaper work suited each other like fish and chips. As a journalist, he could observe people in strange or dramatic situations without becoming personally embroiled, just as he had done in the boys' home, with the eye of a literary voyeur. Life he could view as a sort of great game; he could exist, vicariously, through people and somehow share their experiences. In the same way, he lived *through* literature and not only *for* it. Sometimes he speculated that perhaps he was seeking his unknown self in these characters he created and was compelled to live this sort of second-hand life because he had no antecedents, no genealogy of his own. His behaviour often puzzled him: Why, for instance, he never seemed capable of establishing deep relationships with either men or women, and why he seemed to have no sense of place, no roots. An alien, he belonged nowhere and to no one. On international assignments he felt as much at home in hotel rooms on one-night stop-overs as in his London flat; he walked the streets of Calcutta or Sydney with the same neutral air as he did those of Bermondsey or Kensington. People often branded him, wrongly, a loner and a thick-skinned cynic; in fact he was soft-hearted to the point where he refused to keep dogs, though he loved them, because he would grieve too sorely when they died.

At twenty-two his break came with his second novel, *Not in the Script*. He had marked the fact that so many people, aware or not, were rôle-playing their way through life. Like him, they presented only certain well-rehearsed, carefully scripted versions of themselves to the world. Sent to report the shooting of an American epic film in Spain, Baldwin discovered that some of the leading actors and actresses appeared lost away from the set because they had no lines, no cues; they had to script and direct their own life performances. Outside the nexus of the film set with its actors, directors, writers, cameramen, technicians, they felt lost, inarticulate. Some even larded their talk with bits of dialogue and sounded like reruns of their old movies. Others clung to the clothes and props they used on the set. To Baldwin, they seemed proxy figures, people who were, in a sense, understudying themselves. He heard two big-name actors confess they rejected parts where they had to die, naturally or violently—not through superstition but because scripts often struck them as more real than their own lives. Some swallowed every line of the studio publicity about themselves.

All this inspired *Not in the Script*. Baldwin imagined two stars making a film where the script decreed they should meet and fall in love, putting their broken marriages behind them, renouncing their rich and futile lives and starting afresh. Their film story ended on an idyllic note. However, they took the script too literally and fell in love. They might have lived happily together except that the female star's husband (who had not read the same script) became jealous and enraged. He paid somebody to tamper with the brakes of the car the male star would drive along a cliff in the final, dangerous scene of the film. How could he predict his wife would perish in that car, borrowed by her and her lover for an outing? Life scripts, as the story implied, might come from the pen of God, or the devil.

Not in the Script, with its subtle blend of morality play and violent realism, made Baldwin's name. Now, he could pick and choose his newspaper assignments, and name his own fee. Nine months after publication, the book won the Eddystone Prize, which boosted sales throughout the world. It earned the prize not only for the story and its treatment but also for the powerful writing. Baldwin's newspaper years had taught him how to forge dense and dramatic prose, paring away everything that did not contribute to plot or character. Filing from foreign datelines at so much a word compelled him to use nothing but the most essential words in open-ended sentences, easy to cut or edit. Every perceptive critic spoke of Baldwin's controlled, close-grained style and powerful language and the way he assembled his books with quartz-clock precision.

But in this Irish novel he changed all that. He reread it, first skimming the text, then scanning it, line by line, searching for giveaway tricks of style. He could find none. In fact, he experienced the curious illusion of reading somebody else's work. Maybe because, for the first time, he had told the story through another person's eyes. Even on reflection, he believed neither Dunning, Seaborne, nor any of his critics or readers would recognize it as his. This book had the free-and-easy tone of an Irishman telling the drama over a few glasses of Guinness in the spit-and-sawdust bar of a Belfast pub to half a dozen cronies. But if he had discarded literary tricks and polished prose and tight construction, the novel still had a bitter, earthy sort of poetry. To Baldwin, it read well—but it still had to pass the litmus test of a Belfast man like Gilchrist. Would it fool him?

5

Martin Gilchrist arrived at ten o'clock on the dot. Baldwin had already brewed a pot of coffee and they drank this in the living room with a biscuit while he let his eye skim over the sheaf of stories the Ulsterman had brought. Mercifully, they appeared short and impeccably typed. Nudging them aside, he murmured he would start reading them in a minute or two. From the coffee table by his elbow he lifted his own manuscript, bound in a loose-leaf folder. "Can you keep your mouth tightly shut?" he asked Gilchrist, who looked askance at him, then nodded. "This is my next book," Baldwin continued. "Nobody has seen it or even heard of it or its subject. I'd like you to sit down and read it and tell me, honestly, what you think of it."

"But . . ." Gilchrist's coffee cup rattled nervously in the saucer. He desposited both carefully on the table, staring with puzzled eyes at Baldwin, then shrugging his big shoulders. "But why me? You don't really want my opinion about one of *your* books, do you?"

"I do, and a lot depends on what you think of it."

"Why me?"

"You're an Ulsterman and it's an Irish story."

Gilchrist picked up the script and flipped the folder over to gaze reverentially at the opening paragraphs, read a line or two, then lifted his head. "All right, if you really want me to read it and give my opinion . . ."

"I'll take your stuff into my study and leave you to it," Baldwin said. "You know where to heat the coffee and where the drinks are, and I've cut some sandwiches in the kitchen if you get peckish. Anyway, make yourself at home." He shut the living-room door behind him as he entered his study. There he sat down and opened the file containing Gilchrist's stories and began to leaf through them quickly. They seemed a strange amalgam of simple, direct prose of no particular distinction, though they had one common feature: they read like first-person stories though written in third-person style. Autobiographical, Baldwin assumed. Gilchrist did have something of an eye for a story and a sensitive ear for dialogue as he proved in two cameos of Belfast university life. But one story rang truest. About a young Irish couple whose lives were suddenly changed when they had a mongol child; it shocked both them and their families and led to eternal quarrels and recriminations with everyone denying hereditary blame for such a child. They tried to bring him up as normally as possible, but when the young mother had another child, a girl, she could not manage the mongol boy. After much heart-searching, they found an institution that cared for mentally defective children and placed him there. Neither parent could visit him and look into his vacant eyes without feeling guilty. And when he contracted pneumonia and died eighteen months later, both of them felt like criminals who had committed murder. There was a chance of selling that one, even in the dwindling short-story market, Baldwin reflected.

A couple of hours later, when he had read the lot and passed through the living room to get himself more coffee and a cheese sandwich, he noticed Gilchrist hardly looked up. He was lying with his long limbs speldering over the sofa and he had piled up half the loose typescript pages on the coffee table next to the coffee he had forgotten to drink. A good sign, Baldwin thought. He did not interrupt even when it struck one o'clock and he realized the Ulsterman had eaten nothing. While he waited for the verdict, Baldwin rapped out his comments on the various short stories and pinned them to the folder.

It was just after four o'clock when Gilchrist knocked, tentatively, on the study door, put his head round, then entered. "This is really a terrific book you've written," he whispered, awe in his voice. "Really terrific." His brow knitted as he gazed at Baldwin. "I'd be giving ten years of my life to write a book like that—but to be sure, you didn't need me to tell you this, now did you?" He placed the typescript on the desk.

"What about the dialogue?" Baldwin asked. "I thought my Irishisms might do with a bit of repair in places and you could help."

"A few words here and there where you've used Ulster dialect," Gilchrist said in his strange, soft voice. "But nobody'd notice if you didn't change a thing." Pulling a cigarette out of a crumpled packet, he lit it. "In fact I wondered where you'd been to get the Belfast speech off like that."

"I spent months in Ulster during the troubles."

"Is that where you came across the story? I don't mean to be inquisitive, but it doesn't sound as though you'd invented it all."

"No, it happened a bit like that—but I've made some change in the geography and the plot to protect the real characters." Baldwin indicated a chair. "Take the weight off your legs . . . Martin, isn't it?" Gilchrist nodded and dropped into the armchair. "It kept you turning the pages?" Baldwin asked.

"Unputdownable," Gilchrist exclaimed. "It'll sell in the hundred thousands. And you could film it the way it is, without a scenario." He shook his head in puzzled admiration. "Brilliant, the way you used the IRA man as the narrator." He paused. "I don't know if I should ask you this, but I suppose you met him."

"Somebody who had," Baldwin muttered vaguely. Reaching into his desk drawer, he produced a single page, which he placed on top of the manuscript. "You might have noticed I didn't give you the title page," he said. Gilchrist ran his eye over the six words: *A Common Grave* by Liam Faulds. He shot Baldwin a perplexed glance.

"Liam Faulds," he muttered. "Are you really going to publish a book like this under that pseudonym?"

"That depends on you."

"On me!"

"Let me explain," Baldwin said. "Let's assume I publish the book under my own name—it would make nonsense of the IRA narrator and nobody would believe the story."

"I can see that."

"Another thing," Baldwin went on. "It would become just the latest Graeme Baldwin and everybody would compare it with the last and the one before and in a couple of weeks or a month at the most it would be forgotten."

"Not this book."

"Yes, this book. It would get drowned by phoney best-sellers like *Overrun* and big promotion books and prize novels on which publishers spend most of their ad money."

"How would the pseudonym help that?"

Baldwin lit himself a cigarette and stabbed its glowing end at the title page. "I reckon it would generate interest if I use the name Liam Faulds and leave people to imagine that it's a cover for the IRA man who wrote the manuscript and can't reveal his true identity."

"He can't reveal it! Why?"

"Lots of reasons . . . he might have committed serious crimes . . . left his fingerprints all over a booby-trapped car that killed a policeman . . . and as the book reveals, he sides with his sister, who betrayed the IRA. So, he's on the run from both sides."

"Then I take it he doesn't really exist, this man Faulds," Gilchrist said.

"He doesn't—but nobody can prove that," Baldwin replied. "But we can assume like the readers that the man who wrote this book does exist, he's probably living in Ulster and using the name Liam Faulds as his cover."

"Why are you so keen to keep yourself out of the picture as the author?"

"For the reasons I mentioned," Baldwin said. He paused to give himself time to reflect. "There's another reason. I'd like to rub my publisher's face in the dirt, to show him and my agent I'm not over the hill." He grinned at Gilchrist. "I'd also like to win the Eddystone Prize with the book."

"I didn't think you were keen on prizes."

"Oh, I wouldn't accept it. I'd like to win it merely to announce all my motives for rejecting the honour."

"That would really cause a sensation."

"It would shake a lot of publishers," Baldwin said. "But to get away with all this I need a partner. Somebody I can trust. Somebody like you."

At this, Gilchrist blinked with surprise. "Where would I come in?" he asked.

"You'd represent the man who cannot reveal his name, the man known as Liam Faulds. And for that I'd pay you twenty percent of the book royalties and the same share of the film and TV rights. It could amount to quite a lot of money." Baldwin let that sink home before elaborating; but from Gilchrist's attitude, he could see the project had already appealed to the young Ulsterman. He pressed on with the rest of his argument. "Of course, everything would be legal and foolproof and above board. We'd draw up an agreement, witnessed by a lawyer and placed in his custody, declaring that I would give you twenty percent of my earnings for your help in gathering material or acting as my agent, whichever you decide. We then find a tame Dublin solicitor who'll draw up certain documents, post the manuscript to my publisher and serve as a convenience address. I'll pay him a couple of hundred Irish pounds. He'll have no idea what the script is worth and he'll only know you're acting for somebody calling himself Liam Faulds."

"I don't understand why we need a solicitor, and a Dublin one at that," Gilchrist remarked.

"If you sent it direct, they'd trace it back to you and you'd have to answer too many awkward questions about the man behind Faulds. If we find the right solicitor, he'll draft a convention between you and Faulds without needing to meet him. You get it?" Gilchrist nodded and Baldwin went on, "Dublin's a long way, politically, from Belfast and it's full of solicitors who don't ask silly questions."

"But I don't understand why you want to send it to your own publisher."

"To rub his nose in it," Baldwin replied. "Another thing—if the book fools him, it'll fool anybody. He knows my normal style backwards." He did not mention it would make bookkeeping and the handling of his literary properties easier after the plot was revealed.

"What happens if they find out?"

"They won't—until we're ready to tell them. And that'll be a long time."

"And if they trace the script back to me?"

"You have a story all ready. You were given the manuscript to sell by a friend of the author. From the little you gathered, the man calling himself Liam Faulds is in hiding from the British and the IRA also want to ask him some awkward questions. He's publishing this story to get money to leave the country and settle abroad."

"So, I really don't know the man."

Baldwin nodded confirmation. "All you know is his *nom de plume* and that he's a Belfast Catholic." Baldwin paused, struck by a question. "What are you, anyway?"

"A Catholic, and so's my wife."

"So much the better for your story."

Gilchrist tugged the manuscript towards him and

opened it, thumbing distractedly through the pages for several minutes, obviously turning over in his mind what Baldwin had proposed. "I don't know that it'll work," he muttered, finally.

"It'll work if we follow the plan I've made," Baldwin replied. "Don't forget I'm putting at risk whatever name I've made." Rising, he walked to the study window to gaze at the garden and the rags of sun-rimmed cloud planing over the rooftops. He looked round at Gilchrist. "What's your wife like—I mean, could we trust her to keep the secret?"

"She's a much tougher character than me and I'd trust her with my life," Gilchrist replied with more bite in his tone than Baldwin had heard him use. "Anyway, I'd have to get her go-ahead to come in with you."

"That still makes only four of us in on the secret."

"Who's the fourth?"

"My lawyer, who's bombproof. He's got to draw up the agreement so we know who the real author is and how the money's going to be split."

Gilchrist reached, diffidently, for a cigarette from the chased-silver box on the desk and lit it. Baldwin read doubt in his eyes, as blue as the sunlit smoke spiralling upwards. Had he made a mistake choosing this man as his accomplice without first digging deeply into his background? Yet, Helen Laidlaw considered him a faithful, all-weather friend who had stood by her and Callum in their really desperate days. Callum had never found praise high enough for him, she said. However, Baldwin could not prevent himself from wondering if this soft-spoken Ulsterman would have either the courage or the cunning to deceive an Irish solicitor and the editorial director of a London publishing house. He almost regretted disclosing the scheme without having done more homework on the man. Crossing the study, he slapped Gilchrist on the shoulder. "Look, if you're in any doubt at all, just forget everything you've read and heard and I'll submit the manuscript as I normally do, under my own name but with a preface explaining how I came by the basic story, from a man calling himself Faulds, a relation of the O'Donnell family who does not want his name divulged."

Gilchrist looked up at him, puzzled. "Sorry," he murmured, "my mind was elsewhere. What were you saying?" Baldwin repeated his statement and Gilchrist listened, then shook his head slowly but emphatically. "No, I'd like to go through with it," he said. "It's tremendously exciting and maybe when you decide to tell the truth I'll get a book out of it myself. It would make a book, wouldn't it?"

"A very good one," Baldwin said.

"Only a couple of things bother me," Gilchrist said. "Are we breaking the law . . . I mean, are we guilty of false pretences?"

"Not if we make sure we put nothing in writing and we're vague about where the script came from. People have hidden behind pseudonyms from time out of mind."

"Then all I need is Anne's O.K." Gilchrist said.

With the typescript in his hand, Baldwin led Gilchrist into the living room, where he poured them both a sizable Scotch. "Let's drink to Liam Faulds and *A Common Grave*," he said with a smile. He next went into the kitchen to return with a plateful of sandwiches, apologizing for the plain fare and the fact he could not invite Gilchrist to a restaurant for a meal. "The less we're seen in each other's company from now on, the better," he explained.

Gilchrist bit into a cheese-and-tomato sandwich. "Anne said she'd like to meet you," he remarked. "She's read pretty nearly all your books and was really agog when I told her we'd met at Helen Laidlaw's."

"We must all get together after I fix the lawyer and before we're due to meet him," Baldwin said. "But where?"

"My place," Gilchrist suggested. "It's a third-floor flat in an old building in Fulham. We're in a cul-de-sac and nobody much bothers with us. There, they only read the *Sun* and the *Sporting Life* and you won't be recognized."

Baldwin agreed to see his lawyer, then meet them in a week's time. Before they parted company, he handed the bulky typescript to the Ulsterman. "There's only one other copy," he said. "Don't leave it lying around."

"I'll sleep on top of it."

"Let your wife read it and see what she thinks of the story," Baldwin said. "Then one of you has to sit down and copy the whole thing in longhand. It had probably better be your wife in case somebody just happens to recognize your handwriting—one of your Fleet Street friends, for instance." Witnessing Gilchrist's expression of incomprehension, Baldwin grinned and went on. "It'll look more authentic in longhand, more like the work of a man on the run. Especially if you can remember the sort of school exercise books they use in Belfast schools and buy a pile of those and transcribe the manuscript into them. The grubbier they are, the better."

"Will a publisher even look at a new manuscript in that form?"

Baldwin slapped him on the back again and grinned. "These days they get such beautiful, computerized scripts that ours will create the biggest stir in Gresham and Holt since the Dead Sea Scrolls." Glancing at the other man under his dark eyebrows, he continued, "If your wife's one of those rare women who can spell, tell her to get three or four hundred words wrong—that'll prove Liam Faulds is a natural-born writer, and give their editors something to do."

"Know something?" Gilchrist said, his long face breaking into a beaming smile. "I'm beginning to enjoy this game already."

6

Anthony Raphael Lewis let them into Temple Gardens with his key and they sauntered through the well-barbered lawns, their banks of roses and petunias flaming in the sunlight, down to the Thames embankment, before retracing their way to the corner seat under the Indian bean tree. Lewis glanced several times at Baldwin out of the corner of his eye, thinking how twitchy he seemed as he tapped the end of his cigarette against his thumbnail before lighting the tube and dragging smoke down to his diaphragm; he wondered why the novelist had acted so secretively on the phone, insisting that this interview must take place well away from Lewis's chambers in the Temple. For his part, Baldwin had made the appointment reluctantly, though aware he must. To him, lawyers were a mercenary and mendacious breed; he detested them for their parasitic and Kafkaesque way of battening on their victims, proffering the menace of summary punishment, lost liberty and even death in order to extort high fees. Like those doctors who traded on cancer phobia and other grisly deaths, or grew fat on medical fads. However, he felt he could trust Lewis as far as any lawyer;

he had used him for the divorce wrangle with Diana, then again in an alleged libel and a copyright breach. He was a pouch-faced Jew in his late fifties whose family had changed its name from Levi but had bequeathed him the convex nose, swarthy look and hirsute fingers of some members of his race, plus a slight synagogue intonation. He had the lawyer's habit of trying to throw people off-balance—even outside the courtroom.

"That last book of yours, *A Savage Place*, took a bit of stick," he said.

"Only white stick," Baldwin countered. "What can anybody do about the blind?"

"I read it," Lewis murmured, flicking an insect off his pin-striped trousers. "In all honesty, I didn't care for its story, or its morality. People don't get away with murder."

"People do get away with murder, every day," Baldwin riposted vehemently. "Anyway, the book *wasn't* about a young gigolo who poisoned his wealthy but decrepit old wife, got away with it and married his slut of a mistress. It was about the smell of the sacrificed woman that permeated every room of the mansion they'd taken over and how it poisoned them in their turn and set them against each other." His lip curled as he glanced at Lewis. "That's the trouble with lawyers. You always think justice is a bit of rope or an axe or being plugged into the electricity grid. The answer, my answer, was in the name of the house—Xanadu—and the book's title that came from Coleridge's poem—'A savage place! as holy and enchanted/As e'er beneath a waning moon was haunted/By woman wailing for her demon-lover!'" Baldwin nudged Lewis. "Now do you see?" he asked.

Lewis shrugged, aware he never could win literary arguments with Baldwin and therefore leaving the witness the final word. "What do you want to see me about?" He listened as Baldwin outlined his plan, described his meeting with Gilchrist and the need for a legal agreement, signed and notarized. For several minutes, Lewis turned all this over in his head before looking at Baldwin with bleak eyes. "It's a crazy project," he declared.

"Tony, I didn't come to ask your advice," Baldwin snapped. "Just to pay for your services." From the leather wallet in which he carried his papers, the writer extracted a single sheet in his own handwriting. This he handed to Lewis. It ran:

> I, Graeme Baldwin, forty-four years of age, novelist, of 12 Camden Park Hill, Kensington, and author of the work entitled A Common Grave under the pseudonym, Liam Faulds, hereby agree to pay Martin O'Brien Gilchrist, journalist, of 9 Simon Close, Fulham Road, Fulham, as agent for the said book, twenty percent of all the royalties accruing from the sale of the said book in whatever form, including the audio-visual media, adaptation for the stage, anthology and paperback rights. If it is proved that Martin O'Brien Gilchrist has divulged, or caused to be divulged, the nature of this agreement or the real authorship of the said work to any third party excluding the witnesses of this agreement then it will become null and void.
>
> Signed by both parties on the____day of November 1981 and witnessed by Anthony Raphael Lewis, barrister, and Anne Mahoney Gilchrist, housewife.

Lewis read the paper twice before returning it to Baldwin. "Then you're really serious about this lunatic scheme?" he asked.

Baldwin ignored the question. Instead, he said, "Does that paper legally mean what I intended it to mean?"

"As far as it goes," Lewis replied. "But have you thought the thing through and considered the consequences?" On his hairy fingers, the barrister numbered his objections. "First, your ex-wife could have you thrown in jail for defaulting on your alimony agreement by not declaring and paying her a share of these royalties." At this, Baldwin shrugged his indifference. "Secondly," the lawyer went on, "there's the Inland Revenue, which gets a bit shirty about tax evasion and would slap a fortune in fines on you, and if you couldn't meet them you'd be sewing mailbags."

"We can handle that by getting Gilchrist as Faulds's agent to agree to the publisher's withholding tax on those royalties."

"I suppose so," Lewis conceded. "But there's a third thing—false pretences, though it might be hard to prove."

"Then let them prove it."

Lewis was tapping his fourth finger. "What about this man, Martin Gilchrist? Can you trust him? How well do you know him?"

"Not all that well—but he has good references."

"Have you weighed up the possibility that Gilchrist might blackmail you if the book goes well?"

"I have," Baldwin answered. "He'd be dead stupid if he did, or if he divulged the truth, for he'd automatically lose his twenty percent. Anyway, I know him well enough to realize he's not all that interested in money. He's like me— gone on literature. Something you wouldn't understand."

"I understand human nature," Lewis retorted. "Everybody's interested in money. And anyway, I'm just trying to stop you from committing professional hara-kiri."

"And I'm fighting for my professional life," Baldwin said. "Any other objections?"

Lewis took the short agreement and read it over again, finally folding it, then shaking his head. "Nothing that strikes me offhand. I can tighten up the language and have it typed before we all meet and sign, if that's all right."

"No, it isn't," Baldwin said. "No typists, no fifth and sixth parties who can blab." He reached out a hand and retrieved the paper from Lewis. "If this is a binding document, I shall copy it twice. That makes one for me, one for Gilchrist and the third one for you as the arbiter if either of the parties breaks the contract." With an unsteady hand, he lit his umpteenth cigarette. "And I don't want it kept in the office safe where your clerk has the key."

"I can keep it at home," Lewis said. "I've got my private safe, you know where." For several minutes he watched the half-dozen lawyers with their clients, strolling in the gardens; some wore robes and were obviously stretching their legs between sessions in the law courts. He noticed Baldwin slide the agreement back into his wallet. "How long do you mean to keep this pretence going?" he asked.

"I don't know—I'm interested to see how the whole thing turns out."

"It's more or less a game to you, then?"

Baldwin shook his head vigorously. "It's much more serious than that. You didn't like my last book and a lot of people agreed with your judgement, including my own publisher. You might say this is my way of making a fresh start, a way of sloughing off my old skin." He observed Lewis stare at him uncomprehendingly. How could he explain to this po-faced advocate that even Graeme Baldwin felt like a borrowed name? How to make this man understand that as an orphan he had some sort of psychological impulsion to live through other people and this had transformed him into a novelist in the first place? Even the act of writing that fabricated name, Liam Faulds, on a title page had invented the man for Baldwin and allowed him to step into his character as a turncoat IRA gunman. A lawyer like Lewis, even with his abstract Jewish mind, would never grasp that. He turned to Lewis. "Tony, I have to have somebody I can trust one hundred percent," he said. "Can I count on you?"

"Of course you can," Lewis replied. "But there's a couple of other things you should think about. What happens if you're hit by a truck or your heart stops?"

"You know my literary agent, Harold Seaborne. He'd be handling my literary estate and when he opens my papers he'll get a very red face to discover I'm Liam Faulds."

"A lot of people will have red faces."

"So much the better for you, Tony. You'll earn yourself a fat fee sticking all the broken bits together."

"And Gilchrist—supposing he were to die suddenly?"

"His widow would probably take over his share of the proceeds—but that's up to him. Any more questions?"

Lewis gave a wintry grin. "Only one more," he said. "This book . . . what's it called? . . . *A Common Grave.* I assume it's going to be worth all this kerfuffle."

"If it's not I'll shoot myself," Baldwin said with an unusually bitter note in his voice. "But if I'm still any judge, it's the best thing I've done since *Not in the Script*, and may be even better than that."

"I can't wait to read it," Lewis murmured. "Or to hear the bang it's going to make."

They parted from each other at the northern gate of the gardens. For several minutes, Lewis followed Baldwin's slightly hunched, head-down figure until it disappeared into the labyrinth of twisting alleys leading to Fleet Street, before turning to walk through the gardens to his own chambers. Passing their seat, he glanced at the ring of spent cigarettes, a dozen of them that Baldwin had only half smoked. He knew Baldwin for a brilliant writer, hence a highly sensitive individual liable to swings of mood and emotion. Four years ago, just after his divorce from that frigid bitch of a wife, he had run into what he dubbed a meteor shower and finished up in a depression. He'd swallowed too many pills and they'd had to wash him out in the intensive care unit at Bart's. Or was it Guy's? Then, prickly character that he was, he'd hunted those who suggested suicide, maintaining he'd had too much liquor and it had been a pure accident. Which it might have been. During their three-quarters of an hour together, Lewis had perceived that the twitching, eye-blinking figure of Baldwin was living on a knife edge. Had the lawyer not feared the sort of rough-tongued rebuff the novelist excelled at delivering, he would have hinted that Baldwin might take at least a month's holiday to deliberate more deeply about this quaint charade of his. Although he could not put his finger on it, the barrister suspected a major flaw in Baldwin's scheme. His courtroom sense whispered that the whole plot could easily blow up in the novelist's face.

7

Baldwin had no doubts about either his strategy or the operational details; he had mapped out both, step by step, in the way he plotted his novels. Yet, he realized he still had to organize the trickiest part of the plan—obliterating or covering all his tracks while leaving Gilchrist as little responsibility as possible. After quitting his lawyer, he walked into Fleet Street and the offices of the *Sunday Herald* for which he had often worked on assignment and where he knew the librarian well. For a couple of hours he sat sieving through a pile of newspaper cuttings of IRA cases that had come to trial in Dublin courts; neither the accused nor the charges interested him, merely the names of the solicitors who had acted for the IRA suspects. He finished with a list of five solicitors before consulting the official Eire law list to ascertain which of them acted alone. Law societies might not care for lone solicitors who sought advantages from their privileged position—but secret political and terrorist organisations might. Such legal men did not answer indiscreet questions from publishers, journalists, policemen or anybody else. Baldwin picked two who seemed most likely to have

IRA sympathies: Seamus B. McGirk in Pearse Street and Sean Padraig Ryan in Clanbrassie Street.

That afternoon Baldwin went to his bank in Kensington High Street with the two versions of the manuscript of *A Common Grave*—the story as originally written in the third person, and the photocopy of the script he had given Gilchrist. For all his novels, Baldwin kept every scrap of paper, from the moment he jotted down the source notes to the final word of the final copy; he normally stored these drafts and dossiers in two iron safes in the basement locker room at Camden Hill. Any student or biographer ever attracted to his work would see exactly how he composed his novels. But this script of *A Common Grave* was quite another matter; he decided to place it in his bank strongbox. He followed the bank official through two massive grilles into the basement and waited until the man had turned his passkey in the lock and disappeared before he opened the box with his master key. He inserted the bulky folders with another envelope containing a note to Seaborne explaining everything in case he met with an accident.

That night he flew to Belfast, choosing the midnight plane to lessen the chances of recognition at London Airport; he had already booked into a small hotel off Donegall Road. Later that morning, he walked to Saint Malachy's Catholic Church and asked for Father Regan, waiting by the font until the tall, silver-haired figure appeared and strode down the aisle with his cassock flapping in his own breeze. When Baldwin had researched his series of articles on the Ulster troubles and the IRA, Father Joseph Regan had acted as his guide and mentor through the Roman Catholic districts of Belfast and Derry. A rare priest, he had the respect of both sects; he hailed from Bantry in the extreme southwest tip of Eire and spoke with the soft, susurrating brogue and flowery eloquence of those parts. "Ah, now it's like an eyebath to be seeing you, Graeme Baldwin," he boomed, grasping the novelist's hand in his massive fist. He pulled out a pocket watch. "It's just the wrong side of ten and a mite early, but Paddy that you'll have mind o' will lift the door sneck for two dry-mouthed travellers, will he no' now?" Taking Baldwin's arm, he marched them across Chichester Street to a small pub near Victoria Square, where he ducked along a back alley and knocked on a side door. In a minute, the priest and writer were sitting in a private parlour skimming the creamy foam off two pints of Guinness.

"So, you're after saying this young Irishman who masquerades under the name of Liam Faulds has authored this book about the troubles and is feared to publish it under his own baptismal name."

"From what they tell me he's a man on the run from the British," Baldwin said. "I don't even know where he's living. He gave his manuscript—written in a pile of school exercise books—to a cousin of his who passed it to a friend of his, a certain Martin Gilchrist. He's a Belfast Catholic but lives and works in London. Gilchrist brought the manuscript to me and asked if I could help to get it published." Baldwin halted his explanation for a moment to sip some of his stout, then said, "It's a fine book and ought to be published and widely read not only in Ireland but everywhere."

"And so, if I am to understand the problem . . ." Father Regan began, then paused to allow Baldwin to finish his statement.

"It's like this, Father. Gilchrist needs to have someone vouch that he's the bona fide legal representative of the man calling himself Liam Faulds so that a British publisher will accept the manuscript from him and make a contract to pay him the royalties due to Faulds."

"For my geriatric intellect that's a wee shade convoluted, but I fancy I glimpse what you're intending to mean," Father Regan whispered slowly. From a cassock pocket, he produced a packet of Silk Cut and offered one to the novelist, then lit them both. Baldwin sensed the priest's blue eyes contemplating his face and wondered if all those years in confessional boxes listening to Irish periphrases had developed his sixth sense about falsehood. Finally, Father

Regan spoke. "Now if my poor befuddled cerebrum is not playing me up, I assume you mean this will make it difficult for the authorities to trace the real man behind Liam Faulds."

Baldwin took a long swig of his Guinness and nodded. Like a good Irishman, the priest had no time for the authorities and mistakenly thought Baldwin was taking Faulds's side against them. He felt relieved Father Regan had not tumbled to the fact that attempts to conceal Faulds's identity would have the opposite effect on the public and press. "That's the thing in a nutshell, Father," he murmured. Across the table, he pushed his list of Dublin solicitors with Ryan and McGirk at the top. "If Gilchrist could cross the water and see one of these solicitors and pass the manuscript through him, it would solve the whole problem." As Father Regan looked over the list of names, Baldwin whispered, "Of course, they're all IRA sympathisers, so Gilchrist and Faulds thought they could trust them for that reason."

"If you wish, I can make my own inquiries about their bona fides."

"I'd be grateful," Baldwin said, knowing that throughout Ireland, north and south, the church had a vastly better intelligence service than either the British or the Eire government. "Do you still have occasion to visit Dublin, Father?" he asked.

"You'll be after suggesting I place a personal word for our friends with one of these men," Father Regan said, and Baldwin nodded. For a moment the old priest hesitated. He looked worried. "Now tell me in all truth, Graeme Baldwin, is there anything of the slightest in this book that might cause God's wrath to descend on good Irishmen or on our beloved Mother Church?"

"It's a love story, Father," Baldwin replied. Rapidly, he paraphrased the book and the priest listened attentively, sucking his cigarette and sipping his stout. When Baldwin finished, Father Regan rapped for two more drinks. "I have business in Dublin this coming Monday and I'll pay one or two calls." He pocketed Baldwin's list of legal men. "I take it you'll be here on that evening."

Baldwin thought for a moment. It would allow two days to carry out his bits of reconnaissance; he replied that he would return to Belfast on Monday afternoon and meet the priest at Paddy's pub the same evening.

During the next two days, Baldwin toured Northern Ireland in a hire car, exploring the beautiful, indented coastline from Belfast to Larne and along the Giant's Causeway, making notes and collecting timetables and hotel brochures. He stayed one night in Londonderry before heading for the border county of Fermanagh. His second night he spent in Enniskillen, then motored back through Tyrone and Armagh to Belfast, his wallet full of information that would help Gilchrist when the hunt began for him.

Father Regan had done his duty. "I'm after considering Ryan's your man," he whispered over his Guinness glass. "He has the Irish vices—whisky and horses—and a few others besides that his confessor cannot bear to broach with his cassock buttoned up tight. But Ryan's no man for blarney and he'll traverse fire and brimstone if he thinks—sparing your patriotic feelings—it will bring down the Almighty God of the Irish and Saint Patrick on the English."

"Can we really trust him, Father?"

"Oh, I'm thinking he's a man of his word." Here, the skin crinkled round the old priest's washy-blue eyes. "Ay, even his perjured word—the spalpeen."

8

Baldwin had some difficulty locating the small close at the Thames end of Fulham Road, an enclave of Edwardian buildings in pockmarked, yellowish brickwork that seemed to have developed impetigo from the acid London atmosphere. Gilchrist immediately answered his ring at the street door and preceded him up three flights of stairs to his flat, where he introduced him to his wife. Baldwin had tried to envisage the sort of woman the Ulsterman would have married, but Anne Gilchrist bore little resemblance to his mental portrait. She seemed altogether too fine for the ungainly, big-boned Gilchrist. She had a long, willowy body, perhaps on the fleshy side, set on slender legs; she had firm, high breasts. But it was her face and hair that caught and held his eye. Only two women he had met possessed that kind of tawny hair, this one and Elizabeth Graham, who had brought him up. However, Anne Gilchrist had an altogether stronger face with a straight, tall brow, a slightly tilted nose and full lips. Her upper lip, he noticed, had a little lift, lending her face candour and animation. She had a certain wildness in her expression, a sort of gipsy look he had noticed in some Irishwomen. It appealed to him. Where he had expected blue eyes, hers were brown, a bright, lambent brown, almost chestnut colour. Baldwin became conscious that his scrutiny was perhaps embarrassing her, although she was taking stock of him as well. She smiled and held out her hand. "You're just as I imagined you from the pictures on your book jackets, Mr. Baldwin," she murmured in the same, lilting Ulster intonation as Gilchrist.

"Graeme," he prompted.

"I've read every one of your books except the first one," she went on. "It's out of print and I couldn't get hold of a copy." When they sat down, to prove her statement, she cited several scenes, a dozen characters and even phrases from his books. "You can see I'm a fan," she said, smiling. "But they're all so splendid."

"Including the last one—the typescript I lent Martin?"

"It's not at all like anything you've written before, but I'm sure it's the best thing you've ever done." Her lips parted slightly in a smile. "You know, even after I read it and was copying it I had to stop several times to break the spell. I was away with those Belfast families."

Gilchrist interrupted them to hand Baldwin a Scotch and soda. "But Anne finished the copying, working to all hours of the night," he said. "Do you want to see it?"

"No, Martin," she put in, smiling. "We eat first and discuss all that business afterwards." Gilchrist nodded agreement and Baldwin began to notice the nervous glances he sometimes threw in her direction while they were chatting. In this household, Anne Gilchrist obviously made all the important decisions. Excusing herself, she went into the kitchen to attend to their main course and Gilchrist took the opportunity to show him round the flat with its two bedrooms, kitchen and bathroom. A little girl in pyjamas with straight blond hair and a round, elfin face ran from the smaller bedroom to throw her arms round her father. He kissed her and tucked her back into bed. "That's Moira," he said. "She's six." When they returned, Anne Gilchrist motioned them to the table, where she sat herself between them at the head to enable herself to serve them both. Part of the L-shaped living room did duty as a dining alcove, and she had tricked out the small table with her best cloth, china and cutlery. They ate a quiche Lorraine, probably bought in a delicatessen and heated, then a blanquette de veau with sautéed potatoes, washed down with a cheap rosé wine; they finished with cheese and coffee. During the meal, Anne quizzed Baldwin gently, though only a day or two later did he realize how much of a cross-examination she had put him through. He watched her clear the table, then with those sure hands and blunt fingers dispose the coffee cups and liqueur glasses on the low table before the fireplace. Baldwin opted for Drambuie and accepted one of her cigarettes. "Now, I'd like to hear everything you told Martin last week," she said when they were settled.

Baldwin repeated the whole story, having to backtrack several times to answer her queries. From the way she let her coffee grow cold, the plot was absorbing her, even if she did look dubious when he discussed his motives. Did he really need to resort to such a subterfuge to give his work a new direction or impulsion? Couldn't he just change publishing houses and still write under his own name? Baldwin confessed he wanted to score points off his own publisher to teach them how wrong they were, and the irony of having them publish A Common Grave appealed to him; he wanted to prove to himself he could still hit the best-seller lists without relying on his reputation, and even win the Eddystone or some other literary prize. Finally, she swallowed this. Had he revealed his primary motive—giving himself a new start with a new identity to confer something original on his work—her practical mind would never have accepted it. He described meeting his lawyer and his trip to Northern Ireland, where he had arranged for a Dublin solicitor to act as a post office and guarantor for Gilchrist. Anne took the agreement he had written and scanned it slowly before fixing him with those curious, brown eyes. "It seems in order," she commented.

"It's pretty generous," Baldwin said, and Gilchrist nodded his concurrence.

"This Irish solicitor, Ryan," Anne said. "I suppose Martin will have to go to Dublin to meet him."

Baldwin gave a nod, then added, "He might have to go several times to Northern Ireland to act the part of Faulds's legal representative."

"But somebody's bound to recognize him, either there or here," she objected.

"Not if he watches himself. He can grow a beard, dye his hair black and wear glasses. He can change his voice. And he can meet his contracts well away from his native Belfast."

"He's done amateur theatricals, but I don't know that he'll be able to play this part," Anne mused.

"You see, Graeme, how much faith she has in my acting talents," Gilchrist put in with a laugh.

"You'll do very well," Baldwin said.

"Will he have to use another name?"

"Not with the solicitor. He gives him two hundred pounds and he'll draw up a document stating the man calling himself Liam Faulds, whom he has identified, has appointed Martin O'Brien Gilchrist his agent and representative and conferred on him authority to handle his book, *A Common Grave*, on his behalf." Baldwin turned to Gilchrist. "But in your dealings with the publisher it would be better to use a code name to prevent the press or TV winkling you out."

Anne had retrieved the agreement and was studying it once more. "Is it really worth the risk?" she whispered almost to herself. To Baldwin, she said, "What would a book like this make?"

"Difficult to say—ten thousand pounds at least and up to fifty thousand pounds with all the book rights sold."

"And we'd get a fifth of that—anything up to ten thousand," she murmured.

"Of course, if we sold the film or TV rights, we might double, treble or quadruple those figures," Baldwin remarked.

Anne Gilchrist sipped her Drambuie, then ran the tip of her tongue round her lips as though collecting the residue of the sweet, potent liqueur; her eyes travelled from the scuffed wall-to-wall carpet to the shiny arms and seats of her easy chairs and sofa and finally to the dining-room table as though she were mentally computing what she might do with that sort of money. "I'm just wondering about the snags," she murmured.

Gilchrist had sat silent for a quarter of an hour; now he banged his coffee cup and saucer down on the table. "Look, darling, Graeme's gone over all this with his lawyer, he's spent weeks thinking the thing through and there aren't any snags." Anne shushed him, warning him he would wake Moira, but he continued, though lowering his tone. "Graeme wrote the book, didn't he? He's agreed to cut us in for the reasons he's given and they are good enough for me."

"Do you want me to agree?" she began aggressively, and it looked to Baldwin as though they were going to quarrel. He raised his hand to stop her and turned to Gilchrist.

"Your wife's right, Martin," he said. "If she or either of us sees problems, we've got to sort them out before putting our names to that paper."

At that moment, crying came from the small bedroom. Anne rebuked her husband for waking their child and he disappeared into the bedroom without a word; they heard him comforting Moira. Anne chose that moment to go into the kitchen to heat the coffee and Baldwin rose to stretch his cramped limbs. On the mantelpiece stood two framed photos. One attracted his eye—of Gilchrist and his wife taken perhaps four years before with a small boy aged about four or five standing between them. Even in that small snap, Baldwin discerned the vacant, mongoloid expression and noted the awkward way the boy stood and clung with both hands to his parents. A sudden notion struck him. Was this the boy Gilchrist had written about in that poignant short story of his which Baldwin had assumed to be autobiographical? Pondering this question, he did not hear Anne until she was standing at his elbow and speaking. "That was Michael, our son," she said. "He died three years ago."

"Sorry about that," he muttered.

"We've got over it now," she said. "It was probably better that way. He wasn't quite . . . well, quite right."

Something in her manner and speech set him wondering whether she meant better for the boy, or for herself and Gilchrist. He did not force the point, but sat down while she refilled the coffee cups.

"Exactly how many people know about the nonexistent Liam Faulds?" she asked.

"Only four," he replied. "We three and my lawyer, who will witness our agreement. You'll meet him and you'll agree he's absolutely trustworthy."

"But the Dublin solicitor, Ryan?"

"No problem—he'll only know what he's told and he'll assume Faulds exists somewhere under his real name."

"And the money from the book and other things—how's that paid?"

"Easy. It can go into a numbered account in Switzerland that nobody can trace, and we split it according to the agreement. I can handle all that from this end." At her insistence, he explained how publishers worked, by issuing a cash advance on publication, then preparing royalty statements every six months and crediting the earnings to whatever the author specified. "I'll brief Martin about all this so that he can make these arrangements with the publishing firm."

Anne reflected for several moments, then looked him straight in the eye. "I suppose you've thought what would happen if Martin decided to call the money his," she said. "After all, he's Liam Faulds's sole agent and representative."

"It did cross my mind," he admitted. "He'd merely force me to reveal the true authorship, which I can prove beyond doubt in various ways—by producing the original manuscripts, the signed contract and so on—and you'd lose your share."

Gilchrist returned, having quieted the child and lulled her to sleep. He and his wife exchanged glances and she nodded, almost imperceptibly. "Have we settled all the problems?" Gilchrist asked, and the others affirmed they had.

Now it was Anne's turn to rise and disappear into the larger bedroom and come back carrying a pile of exercise books nearly eighteen inches high, plus the original typescript of *A Common Grave*. She handed Baldwin several of the school jotters and he flipped through them, marvelling at the professional job she had done. These would have fooled anybody. Anne had changed pens every ten or twenty pages, using blue, black and even red ballpoints; she had misspelt a good many words and on every page had scored out a line or two, rewriting these in the margin. Baldwin congratulated himself on choosing her for a collaborator. Even the script looked authentic with its rococo whorls and loops. "They're the kind of jotters they still use in Ulster schools," she commented. "And Martin and I roughed them up a bit so they'd think the story had taken months to write and had been done in a shabeen by the light of a peat fire." She smiled, pointing at the rings left on several pages by a tea mug. "They're authentic," she said. "I drink a lot of tea."

"You've quite a flair for this sort of work," Baldwin remarked. "Maybe I should have made you Liam Faulds's agent, and not Martin."

When he had examined the twenty-one school jotters, Gilchrist asked if he wanted his own typescript back; he said yes, and Anne went to wrap it up. He explained to both of them where his lawyer lived in Bayswater, saying they had arranged to meet there rather than at his chambers, where his clerk and secretarial staff might remember them. In a couple of days' time they could sign the paper with Anthony Lewis witnessing and certifying the document. Gilchrist could then fly to Belfast for a visit to his home town; from there he would take the train to Dublin and hand over the twenty-one exercise books to Ryan, the solicitor. Baldwin would write out a set of instructions for the Ulsterman, who would memorize them, then destroy the paper.

Walking from the close to Parsons Green tube station, Baldwin sensed a sort of elation at the way his plan was progressing. That meeting had comforted him; he might have picked much worse than the Gilchrists for accomplices. Quite a girl, Anne Gilchrist. And Gilchrist was a lucky man to have somebody like her back-stopping him. He wondered how Dunning and his brood would react when those exercise books landed on their desk. What if they just chucked them all back as so much trash? That small doubt niggled at Baldwin's mind as he sat among the late-night travellers in the Underground. But then, every book he had written—even the best-sellers and those the critics had raved about—had aroused the same misgivings.

Only when he left the train to walk up Camden Hill did he realize he had left the typescript of A *Common Grave* behind. That chafed at his mind, too, for it could mean that, subconsciously, he wanted another invitation to the Gilchrists, and not to see Martin.

9

To occupy his hands and mind and restrain himself from imagining Gilchrist in Dublin tumbling into all kinds of elephant traps of his own making, Baldwin wrote a short narrative in diary form to record his reasons for this complicated masquerade and each step in the conspiracy. He remembered one critic—was it that hornless old cow, Cecilia Parkstone?—declaring that Graeme Baldwin reflected and wrote like an author with no antecedents, literary or social, but who desperately wanted a toehold on posterity. For once, she might have chanced on the truth. Anyway, if the story evolved as he anticipated, it would make fascinating reading in twenty years' time for some biographer or literary sleuth. A novel arising out of a novel arising out of a novel! The more he reflected the more he realized he could even use the plot he had conceived and the characters—himself, Anne and Martin Gilchrist, Dunning, Lewis—to write yet another novel. With Gilchrist, Dunning and Lewis he'd have no difficulty. Straight men, all of them. But Anne! Even from the few hours he had spent observing her he could judge how tricky she might prove to put down on paper; she seemed so full of Irish temperament and subtle mental twists. She'd take some knowing. And himself? To portray himself objectively, as a third-person character, he'd hardly know where to begin. He was a real chameleon on tartan, changeable, perverse, wearing a dozen face masks.

A week after they had signed the agreement and three days after Gilchrist had flown to Dublin via Belfast, Baldwin's phone rang. Anne did not need to announce herself since her Ulster accent took care of that. She had ordered the goods, which were on the way to London by registered post; she had contacted the sender, who had assured her he had completed all the necessary customs clearance forms with the required two signatures and had steered the package through the post himself. His only worry: Should he wait there until the package had arrived and been acknowledged?

"Yes, tell him to wait there for three or four days in case we have a query this end when the package is opened," Baldwin said, impressed with her cover story. "Has he got a number where I can reach him if necessary?" She gave him the number of the small Dublin hotel where Gilchrist was staying under the name of Michael Murphy.

"When I have mind of it, you left something in our place the other evening—a package. Did you want it?"

"I'm sorry, I need it," Baldwin replied. "I can come over tonight or tomorrow night and pick it up, if that's all right with you."

"No, don't do that," she said quickly, then added, "I mean I don't know if I'll be in tonight. Hold on a second." She went silent for a little while, then said, "Can you meet me at lunchtime tomorrow? Just after one? Along Chiswick High Road there's a pub called the Cross Keys. I'll bring it there."

Baldwin agreed to this arrangement, though wondering if this were not carrying her cloak-and-dagger style a bit far. Or if Anne Gilchrist had a lover tucked away somewhere. Yet he also had to question his own attitude. Why had he suggested postponing Gilchrist's stay in Dublin? He knew that Gresham and Holt or any other publisher might take at least a month to deliberate over the manuscript—even if convinced that those twenty-one exercise books contained potential best-seller material. No good his conscious mind telling him he was merely taking precautions against the fact that someone in Gresham and Holt might try to contact Gilchrist when the manuscript landed. His inner mind was whispering more honestly that he was seeking another opportunity of meeting Gilchrist's wife on her own.

He got to the Cross Keys just before one o'clock to find its saloon bar jammed tight with lunchtime customers; he therefore chose the quieter spit-and-sawdust bar and a corner seat where he sipped a beer and read the *Daily Mirror*. Five minutes later he saw Anne arrive and scan the saloon-bar crowd before spotting him and making her way round the barrier. To his surprise, he noted she was wearing white cotton stockings and white canvas shoes with thick rubber soles. Baldwin went to fetch her the lager she wanted. "Why don't you let me buy you lunch somewhere?" he proposed.

"No time. I'm due back at two on the dot."

"Due back where?"

"Charing Cross Hospital." She sat down and pushed the manila envelope containing the typescript across the small table at him, then took off her coat and flung it over the seat back. She smiled at him, then pointed a finger at her white-clad leg. "I'm a working lass, didn't you know?"

Baldwin shook his head. "Doing what?" he said.

"I'm a medical secretary on the surgical wards."

"Martin didn't say anything about it," Baldwin muttered.

Her laugh rang round the small bar. "No, he wouldn't let that out," she exclaimed. She lit a cigarette and said through the smoke, "Anyway, what made you pick Martin?"

"I don't really know," Baldwin replied. "He's got this obsessive yen to be a writer, and I thought the scheme would appeal to him."

"That's not all, surely."

She had her brown eyes fixed on him and Baldwin had to remember he was dealing with an Irishwoman who looked as though she had a sixth sense that could probe his unspoken mind. "No," he conceded after a moment. "It seemed to fit together, the whole scheme. I was mad at the Eddystone jury for turning down Callum Laidlaw and wanted to get my own back on them and take a sideswipe at my publisher. And at Helen Laidlaw's there was your husband. I remembered him when I saw something on the TV box a night or two later that triggered off the idea of inventing a new writer and making a new start. I had a script almost completed with the Irish background—ready-made for Liam Faulds, and your husband." Baldwin paused before adding, "Of course, I reckoned I could trust Martin."

"You can," she said. "He couldn't go through customs with an extra packet of fags." She narrowed her eyes to gaze across at the blackboard with that day's pub lunch chalked on it. "What do you fancy?" she asked. "Ploughman's bread and cheese, a Scotch egg or bangers and mash?"

"I'll get them," Baldwin said.

"Bangers and mash for me, then."

Pushing through the crowd to the bar, Baldwin returned with sausages and mash, mustard, two wedges of Cheddar cheese and butter, two feet of French bread; he also fetched two more lagers. Anne picked up the sausage with her fingers, incised its end and wrenched it off with her strong teeth, trowelled butter on her bread, chewed some with the sausage, then swallowed some beer. Her vitality impressed him. "Do you like working at Charing Cross Hospital?" he asked.

"Better than housework and minding the kid," Anne said through another mouthful of sausage. "I've always worked, from fifteen onwards. I was a trained nurse, a blue belt at the Royal Victoria in Belfast before I came over here." She made it sound like some top grade in judo. Flicking tawny hair off her face, she flashed him an arch look. "It's where I met Martin, the Royal Vic—the day he was brought in with a cracked skull from the rugger pitch. I still blame myself for what I did to pull him round. When we fight, I tell him he never fully got over that crack on the head."

"It must be pretty hard, working and keeping a home going."

"How would we have survived without me earning money?" She sighed. "You've met Martin, and well . . . he tries, but . . ." She elided the thought, leaving him to finish it.

"What happens to Moira when you're at the hospital?"

"She goes to an infant school in Fulham and a neighbour picks her up and takes care of her until I get back. On no-school days I place her in a local crèche." Halfway to her mouth with a piece of bread loaded with cheese, she suddenly stopped and fastened her brown eyes on his face. "Why are you staring at me like that?" she demanded.

"Was I staring?" he muttered. He must have been un-consciously studying her face, perhaps pondering how best to describe it. Or he might have been trying to analyze her. Often he caught himself running over this or that phrase, applying it to people who attracted him or, in this woman's case, fascinated him. "I'm sorry if I was rude," he said.

"No, it wasn't rude." Her eyes and mouth crinkled at the corners. "It was . . . well, maybe even flattering."

"It couldn't be anything else," he said. "You're a very lovely woman, Mrs. Gilchrist."

Abruptly, she threw her head back and laughed, the sound bubbling in her exposed throat and escaping through parted lips and rising above the clamour of the pub. "Mrs. Gilchrist," she repeated and laughed out loud again. "Surely, you can call me Anne." She gazed at him, still smiling. "After all, we're a couple of fellow conspirators—or had you forgotten?"

"All right, Anne," he said. For several minutes they sat silent, finishing their snack. Baldwin produced cigarettes and they smoked. Even then, he could not resist scrutinizing her almost like some heroine for one of his novels. He noted the way the lime-green silk blouse set off her titian hair and brown eyes, obviously chosen for that purpose. Open-necked, it revealed enough of the cleavage and curve of her breasts to tease his interest. He noticed, too, the golden aura of nicotine overlaying the index and third finger of her right hand. And how curiously spatulate the finger ends seemed. How cruel! Was that the word? He stubbed out his cigarette. "I'd like to know more about you," he said.

That notion she dismissed with a throwaway gesture of her hand. "You're the interesting person in the plot—not me," she said. "Anyway, what were you going to do—put me between the pages of a book?"

"No, I was just intrigued, that's all."

Anne evidently did not wish to continue this line of talk; she pointed her cigarette at the envelope concealing the manuscript of *A Common Grave*. "Do you think it will do well, your book?" she asked.

"Books are nearly always a bit of a lottery."

"When I was copying it, I was amazed at the stuff you'd discovered on the IRA. Where did you come by all that information?"

"I spent several months in the battle zone between the Falls Road and Shankill Road doing an in-depth series of articles for the *Sunday Herald*." He shrugged. "It's not too difficult for a professional illusionist like me."

"You're too modest," she said. "You've done just about everything."

"I've written nineteen published books," Baldwin replied. "All the rest—the travel, the adventure, meeting the so-called famous—doesn't mean that much once you've done it."

"But you've done it," she murmured, her gaze far away. "I'll never get the chance."

"You will, if *A Common Grave* gets into the best-seller lists."

She turned that thought over in her mind, her eyes pensive, her cigarette dropping ash. "Funny," she mused. "I was thinking, this scheme of yours—it's just like the plot you might have used in one of your novels."

"True," he conceded. "Only I usually know the end of my stories before I write the first line and some of my books are written backwards—from the last page to the first. Here, I don't know the ending."

"Isn't that what makes it so exciting?" she said. "I never want to know how tomorrow will turn out. It would take all the fizz out of life for me."

They sat there, now silent in the swirl of pub noise and smoke and movement as if they could both sense a subtle, unspoken complicity between them, as if the conspiracy they had created was drawing them closer together. Suddenly, Anne looked at her watch and stubbed out her cigarette. Getting to her feet, she drained the dregs of her lager standing up and announced she must run. When he made to follow her, she stopped him with an upraised hand. "Give a ring when it's all right for Martin to fly back," she whispered in his ear, then hurried from the pub.

Baldwin watched her from the window until she vanished between the tall buildings. He felt lonely, and wished he were ten years younger, or even five. Aware the day had lost its point and he might as well dismiss any idea of work, he wandered sadly back through Hammersmith to Kensington. He placed the typescript with the other manuscripts relating to *A Common Grave* in his bank deposit box, then went to a cinema to while away several hours until he could go to his club and have dinner.

10

A week later, Keith Dunning invited him to a board-room lunch, insisting he arrive around midday to discuss something important. "A very private job, ol' boy, very hush-hush." Already one move ahead of the publishers, Baldwin rang Gilchrist advising him to pack a bag and prepare to fly to Northern Ireland and remain there for anything up to three weeks. Baldwin arrived at the Gresham and Holt headquarters near Covent Garden ten minutes late, purposely, to make his editor sweat. Dunning drew him into his office, shut the door, pulled the plug out of the intercom machine and lit a cigarette with trembling fingers. "What's all this undercover stuff?" Baldwin said, grinning. "You look as though they're after you."

"Look, Graeme, try to be serious for once," Dunning whispered. "There's something I want you to study closely." From a desk drawer he extracted two of Anne Gilchrist's exercise books and thrust them at Baldwin, who thumbed the pages, then gazed at the editor with raised eyebrows. "We've got another nineteen like that," Dunning said in his ear. "Read two or three pages."

Baldwin complied, pretending to read the scene where Kathleen O'Donnell and Hugh Montgomery declared their love. Dunning sat smoking nervously. After ten minutes, Baldwin threw down the jotter. "I can't read stuff like that," he lamented.

"You don't like it!" Dunning said, anxiously.

"It's all right—but that schoolboy handwriting gives me the gears. Haven't you got a decent typescript?"

Dunning reached into another drawer and produced a pile of typed paper. "Look, I'll give you three-quarters of an hour to read what you can. I want your considered opinion. It's important."

Left alone, Baldwin turned the pages, though focussing his mind on what to tell the directors. After all, they might recall the lunchtime dialogue if the book were traced to him, or he chose to reveal his literary confidence trick. They would hardly appreciate being duped, especially if their rivals blamed them for pulling a sales and publicity stunt with Baldwin's connivance.

Dunning returned. "What do you think, then?" he asked.

"Not bad," Baldwin conceded. "Of course, it's an Irish variant of *Romeo and Juliet*, but you've published worse."

"We think it's brilliant."

"Who's this man Faulds—another genius from the Belfast slums or the bogs of Sligo?"

"We don't know." Dunning's neck twitched.

"What do you mean, you don't know?"

Dunning explained that the school jotters had dropped on their desk a week ago with a covering note from a Dublin solicitor called Ryan who claimed the author's authority to act for him. For private reasons, the author was using the *nom de plume* Liam Faulds; however, he had appointed a proxy, empowered to represent him in everything. This was a man named Michael Murphy, a Northern Ireland citizen. Ryan had drawn up an agreement between Faulds and Murphy which the publisher might consult. Proceeds from the story would be paid to Murphy for transmission to Faulds.

"So, I take it Liam Faulds is the narrator of this story," Baldwin said, pointing to the script. "And that very likely means he's a man on the run."

"Roughly what we thought," Dunning said. He mopped his perspiring cheeks with a silk handkerchief, and Baldwin reflected that no editorial director with an Eng-Lit degree and a thousand books under his belt should have to take such life-and-death decisions.

"Of course, a book like this is bound to get published," he said. "Chuck it back, and it'll go to any one of half a dozen big publishers.

"And they've given us only a fortnight to decide."

Dunning steered him into the Georgian boardroom where the three other directors were drinking aperitifs. He already knew the managing director, Roger Hanbury-Giles, a plethoric former salesman with a taste running to pulp fiction and potted biographies. He buttonholed Baldwin to fling several questions about *A Common Grave* and its mystery author.

"Why does everybody want my opinion?" Baldwin said. "I thought I was a washed-up writer on your back list."

"You'll make your comeback," Hanbury-Giles retorted. "We here still consider you one of our top authors."

Dunning pushed between them a whisky for Baldwin. "The managing director felt you were the best man to ask because of your literary judgement and because you spent months in Ulster and know all the background to the Faulds book."

"Exactly," Hanbury-Giles snapped. "Is this book authentic, Baldwin?"

"I haven't read it all, so how would I know?"

"Just give us your first impressions," Hanbury-Giles insisted.

"I'd say it was genuine," Baldwin replied. "It's difficult

80

to invent that sort of first-person story and make it ring true."

"When you were in Northern Ireland, did you hear of stories like this star-crossed romance between the O'Donnell girl and the Montgomery boy?"

Baldwin nodded. "At least half a dozen like it."

"What's your view on the way this man, Faulds, is trying to sell us his book?"

"He's got good reason to protect himself," Baldwin said cryptically.

"I've told Baldwin something of the background given us by the solicitor," Dunning interjected.

Baldwin was conscious of all three directors staring at him, waiting for his verdict. "I'd say Faulds, or whatever his real name is, has had trouble either with the British authorities or he's a renegade IRA man and may still be close to that organization."

"As a writer, what do you think?" Hanbury-Giles asked.

"If this is a first novel, then he's something of a genius," Baldwin replied.

They sat down to prawn cocktail, Dover sole and cheese, liberally irrigated with vintage white wine from the firm's cellars. Baldwin found himself the target of four lines of crossfire about *A Common Grave*. He was revelling in this situation, full of irony. Wouldn't he love to see those four faces when they discovered Liam Faulds was their own spurned Graeme Baldwin? And they would. For even now he was noting their remarks about Faulds and his novel to put them in his own book about the Faulds affair. It was not only Dunning who acted like some cornered spy. Hanbury-Giles waited until the waiters had disappeared before turning to Baldwin with his booming whisper. "One question bothers the lot of us," he intoned. "If this man, Faulds, turns out to be an IRA criminal who's still part of the organization and he uses the royalties we pay him to buy guns and bombs to kill Ulster policemen, British soldiers and innocent civilians, we're all going to look a real bunch of nits and ninnies, aren't we?"

Baldwin agreed, pretended to reflect for a moment, then said, "If you're worried, why don't you send Dunning over to Dublin to meet this solicitor and get a written guarantee from him and Faulds's representative—this man Murphy— that the money's not going into the IRA's funds?"

"Dunning, why didn't we think of that?" Hanbury-Giles barked. "Have we got an address for Murphy?"

"We can contact him through the solicitor," Dunning mumbled, shooting a narrow-eyed look at Baldwin. He did not appreciate either the rebuke or the idea of getting embroiled even with fringe IRA gunmen.

"I'd get on the first plane to Dublin tomorrow," Hanbury-Giles said. "The quicker we tie this man up, the better." A thought flashed over his ruddy face and he looked round the table. "Just off the top of my head, wouldn't it be a good ploy to get Baldwin, with his name and his inside knowledge of Northern Ireland, to write a foreword to the book when we decide to publish?"

"Splendid idea, sir," the publicity director said, and Dunning and the other director both nodded.

Baldwin pushed out his lips and shook his head, slowly. "If I write a foreword and the book's a winner and comes up for the Eddystone, as a member of the jury my hands will be tied and I won't be able to do a thing to lobby it through." He paused, then added, "Anyway, I doubt if Dunning would get Faulds to agree to such a foreword."

They drank their coffee, reflected and dismissed the notion. As they broke up, both Dunning and Baldwin were sweating. It would have looked odd in posterity's eyes had he written a eulogy about his own work. Dunning led him back to his office.

"Of course, everything you've heard here is under our hats, Graeme," he said.

"I can keep the secret." He glanced at Dunning's miserable face and could not resist saying, "If I were you, I'd choose a hotel well away from the Falls Road and Shankill Road—those bombs and rifle fire keep some people awake." As he left the building, Dunning was phoning Dublin trying to make an appointment with Ryan and his secretary was booking his flight. Poor Dunning! Little did he know the trip Baldwin had prepared for him.

At ten o'clock that night when he answered a knock at his door, Baldwin did not recognize the figure on the step. It was Gilchrist. He was wearing a dark, bushy beard and moustache and had a dark wig on his head. He looked like a picture of the young Tolstoy in his Crimean days. Baldwin pulled him inside and banged the door shut. Under the living-room lights he scrutinized him. "What's the Old Vic get-up for?" he asked.

"It's the disguise I'm going to use to meet Dunning," Gilchrist muttered somewhat apologetically. "Anne said if it passed muster with you it would fool people, even them that know me, the other side. And you mentioned yourself, the less we were seen together—"

"You're right," Baldwin cut in. "And it's effective, I must admit."

"I've got a couple more changes," Gilchrist said, whipping a pair of heavy, tortoise-shell glasses out of his pocket.

"What does Anne think of all this?"

"She's the one that thought it all up." Gilchrist chuckled. "You know, we used to star in amateur theatricals in Queen Victoria Hospital—shows for students and patients."

"That is a bit more serious," Baldwin said.

"We know that and we've both spent hours rehearsing every single instruction you've given us."

Baldwin poured them whiskies and outlined his meeting with Dunning and his directors. "They've guzzled the bait—hooks and all. Now it's only a question of gaffing Dunning." In graphic language, he explained Dunning's dry, ascetic character. "We give him the runaround, scare the hell out of him and, if I know him, he'll fancy the whole of the IRA's on his back and he'll sign the contract double-quick." He took Gilchrist step by step through all the moves, insisting he act like an IRA man and haggle over the contract to get the best possible deal.

"But Graeme, I know nothing at all about book contracts."

Baldwin produced a photocopy of his own contract for *A Savage Place* and handed it to the Irishman. "That'll teach you all you have to know," he said. "Study the royalties clauses and the various rights publishers and authors split between them and get the same, or better." Dunning would have the authority to change the terms.

He replenished their glasses and lit another cigarette. "One thing I must ask you," he said. "Dunning knows you as Michael Murphy. But I don't think you can sign the contract as Murphy if you've already drawn up an agreement with Ryan using your own name."

Gilchrist gulped his whisky. He looked embarrassed. "I meant to tell you about that," he muttered. "You see, Anne and myself decided it might be too dangerous using my own name. I'm too well known around Belfast. I should've phoned from Dublin to clear this, but I felt I had to call myself Murphy in front of Ryan. What I did to prove my real identity was sign myself Murphy over my palm and fingerprints." From his briefcase, he pulled out a copy of the contract, which Baldwin scanned before filing it.

"Just don't run into anybody who knows you when you're using the name Murphy."

"No problem," Gilchrist said, grinning. "My best friends walked past me yesterday when I tried out this disguise. Of course, I changed my voice and my accent." There and then, he switched from his Belfast brogue into softer, Dublin speech, did a North Country accent and an Oxford drawl.

Baldwin was impressed. "But Ireland will be trickier," he said. He rose, went to a drawer and brought out a bundle of ten-pound notes, which he tossed across the table to the Ulsterman. "You'll need cash for at least a couple of weeks and your air fare. There's three thousand pounds in that lot. If you need more, phone Anne and we'll wire you money in Murphy's name." He raised his whisky glass. "Here's hoping there are no snags."

"Don't worry," Gilchrist said. "I'm just crossing my fingers the book does as well as I think it should."

That phrase echoed in Baldwin's mind long after the Irishman had gone. Gilchrist had given it a curious, proud ring as though he had written the book. At any rate, he appeared to identify completely with the story and its fake author. It would help to make the masquerade stick. Yet, it was strange, Baldwin reflected. You create something and put a new name on it, and that new name seems not only to change the object but to transform in subtle ways the people who created it. He'd better watch out himself, or he'd begin to imagine Liam Faulds actually existed and Gilchrist, alias Michael Murphy, really was Faulds's agent and proxy. He was beginning to wonder if that book, designed to boost his literary career, might not transform his existence as well as the Gilchrists'.

11

Dunning was cursing the day *A Common Grave* landed on his desk. It had taken three days of phone calls to persuade that drunken Irish solicitor to contact Murphy. Then Murphy rejected any idea of a face-to-face meeting. Wouldn't he be trusting an honest Dublin lawyer to make the contract? Dunning argued he had vital problems to discuss in person or he could not accept the novel. "All right, chuck it back and I can find another book firm," Murphy's twangy voice shouted over the spitting line. However, Dunning wheedled and cajoled until the man agreed to see him. But on conditions. He should go by train to Stranraer in southwest Scotland and catch the Larne steamer. "But I can fly from London to Belfast in an hour," Dunning grumbled.

"And bring a pack of reporters with you," Murphy replied. "If anybody tries to photograph or trace Liam Faulds, I withdraw the script and the deal's off."

"I shall respect Mr. Faulds's anonymity," Dunning said loftily.

A day later at Larne, when Dunning phoned for new instructions, he was ordered to hire a car, drive to Ballycastle and take a boat to Rathlin Island. In pelting rain, he followed coast roads that seemed to be toppling into the sea; at the small port, he had to bribe a boatman to make the eight-mile crossing in a heavy swell that threatened to swamp the motor launch. He arrived sodden, shivering; in the island's one inn, they poured him a double whisky to resuscitate him. "You'll be a Mr. Dunning, will ye no'?" the landlord asked. "A chentleman booked you in. You'll be biding here till he's telephoning you."

For two interminable days, Dunning kicked his heels on the island, anchored between Scotland and Ireland, inhabited by a handful of fishermen and farmers, several thousand sheep and swarms of seabirds. Rathlin had provided sanctuary for Scotland's hero king, Robert the Bruce, until he was inspired by a spider to go back and beat the English. It wasn't the spider, Dunning reflected, but this treeless, gale-swept hell. He was growing sick of the staple fish and chips when Murphy rang on the second night. Now satisfied Dunning was alone, they could meet. He would pick up his car, drive across Ireland to Strabane near the Republic border and book into the Nelson Hotel. Only the dread of seeing Faulds a best-seller elsewhere prevented Dunning from throwing in his hand. Murphy instructed him to drive down the border road to an inn called the Sion Arms. He would be waiting there from eight o'clock and the landlord would know him by the name Sean Carey.

What was Murphy doing, luring him into IRA country? Dunning's imagination, fed on more than ten years of senseless and vicious murder and maiming, torture and bombing, got the better of him. Even his Rathlin boatman looked like an IRA killer. On the long and lonely drive through Antrim, Londonderry and Tyrone counties, every wood concealed an IRA hit squad, every pothole racketed in his car and body like an exploded mine. After dark, peering into his headlights for road mines and armed men, he drove the last five miles at a crawl. Just before eight he stopped outside the Sion Arms in a hamlet south of Strabane. It looked no more than a crofter's cottage converted into a pub. When he edged, apprehensively, inside it seemed every eye fell on him, everything hushed and even hands halted halfway to mouths with whisky or Guinness. A centipede with electric legs paraded along Dunning's back. Fear almost turned him round and set him fleeing. After all, what was a strange face in an English suit doing in a sleazy pub several hundred yards from one of the most troubled borders in the world? He read the same idea in that ring of white faces, like onions on a string, suspended in a tobacco-smoke fug and peat reek from the fire. To them, he could only be a spy, a member of the SAS undercover group, or at best a plainclothes policeman. They stared at his leather briefcase, for in that part of Ireland every parcel or package contained a bomb until contrary proof. Dunning glanced nervously at the whisky-faced landlord behind the corner bar, then searched the faces of the dozen-odd customers; in the buttery light from one bulb that was threatening to give up the struggle against the fug, he discerned no one who looked like Murphy among the men in hookerdoon caps and open-necked shirts. As he turned, finally, to speak to the landlord, a hand clutched his arm, a black-bearded, bespectacled face approached his ear and a voice whispered, "Mr. Dunning, is it not?" Numbly, he followed the man into a corner and, to his relief, several voices broke the silence.

"So you're Mr. Michael Murphy," he whispered.

"No, I warned you, I'm Sean Carey."

"You're not Liam Faulds, then?"

At this, Dunning saw his companion clench his big fist. "Don't for Christ's sake and the sake of Mary, Mother of God, mention that name. People in these parts have good memories." With a raised finger, he checked the retort on Dunning's lips. "What'll ye be after drinking?" he asked. Dunning muttered he wanted a whisky. Following his Rathlin ordeal and that spooky drive, he felt in need of a stiffener. Murphy returned with two large Bushmills whiskies and two glasses of Guinness, hissing they should wait until the music started before talking. Within a few minutes, a man who had been sitting by the fire cradled a melodeon on his knee and struck up an air which another man began to sing:

> *"She is far from the land,*
> *Where her young hero sleeps . . ."*

Dunning did not know much Irish history, but he seemed to recognize the ballad as a lament for the first Irish political martyr, Wolfe Tone. Gulping a large mouthful of whisky, he whispered, "Can we get down to things now?" Gilchrist nodded, and the publisher went on, "Who exactly is this man, Liam Faulds? We want to know. We must know."

"Then you'll be having to go and be asking himself that question," Gilchrist said in his thick Irish brogue. "I don't know, for sure."

"But you must have some idea!"

"That I have not and I am not wanting to have for my own head's sake," Gilchrist said, stressing the last phrase. "I got them schoolbooks from a person calling himself a cousin of Faulds who was only asking me to sell the story and take ten percent commission." Gilchrist swallowed some whisky and grinned. "I read the book myself and didn't think it worth much."

"But why did they choose you?"

Gilchrist reflected for a moment, cocking his head as though listening to the ballad. He said, "How would I be knowing that thing, by the grace of Saint Patrick? Mebbe he pulled my name out of a hat. Mebbe I was at school with Faulds. I am just not knowing."

"But you've met him . . . you must have . . . through this solicitor, Ryan, in Dublin."

Gilchrist shook his head. "No, I did not," he said. "Faulds is too clever and too scared. He had Ryan take our statements separately."

"So, what does that mean?" Dunning queried. "He's on the run from the British, or the IRA? Or he's still in the IRA?" At this question, Gilchrist shrugged as though this mattered little to him; he rose and sauntered to the bar to return with the whisky and Guinness glasses full. "That's what worries my firm," Dunning insisted. "Suppose the royalties from this book—if we publish it—go to the IRA. You can imagine the stink that would cause in Britain."

Gilchrist sipped his black stout and lit a cigarette. "I don't think he's an IRA gunman," he said. "From what I gather, he wrote the story to get enough money to leave Ireland, and don't be asking me why for I am just not knowing."

"But we must be sure he's not a criminal on the run, a murderer maybe, or an IRA terrorist," Dunning said. He realized that, in his nervous panic, he had swallowed his second double whisky and half his second Guinness. Three men were now crooning another ballad and the words and the melodeon tune were resonating and jangling in his head:

"Oh, from sweet Dungannon to Ballyshannon,
From Cullyhanna to oul' Arboe,
I've roved and rambled, caroused and gambled,
Where songs did thunder and whisky flow."

"Mr. Ryan assured me on his professional oath, on Saint Patrick's head and the Holy Book, Faulds was not a wanted man or an IRA man," Gilchrist said. "If you are so wishing to do, you can go and confirm this with him."

"I've met him and he gave me the same guarantee and I've already written this into the contract," Dunning said, aware he was now slurring his words and finding mental concentration difficult. Had this massive, black-bearded villian opposite him slipped something into the whisky? Glancing furtively around, he wondered why this Murphy or Carey or whatever had chosen this remote pub near the Eire border. Probably to flee to the Irish Republic if the Ulster police or

British troops raided the place. Those rugged, unkempt figures with rough clothing and scowling looks might easily be IRA men who had slipped across the border to act as his bodyguard. "Can you read in this light?" he asked. But as he made to produce the contract from his briefcase, Gilchrist leaned over to clamp a ham hand over his wrist.

"Leave that where it is," he said in a grating whisper. "No papers in a place like this. And keep your hands out of your pockets." He glanced towards the landlord who, Dunning fancied, had his bloodshot eyes on both of them. His companions must have made some signal, for the landlord crossed the room with two more whiskies and Guinnesses.

"I couldn't conceivably drink that," Dunning gasped. Apart from a sandwich he had eaten nothing all day and the two whiskies and stouts had already set his head gyrating and the hot fug and tobacco smoke and peat reek lay on his chest like mustard gas.

"They'd wonder, if you were after leaving it," Gilchrist murmured, flicking his eyes at the ring of men. "Tell you what, drink the whisky and I'll finish the Guinness for you." Reluctantly, Dunning complied. A warm, wet numbness was creeping over him.

"Don't you want to read and sign the contracts I've drawn up?" he asked thickly.

"We'll discuss those things seriously when we're getting back to your hotel in Strabane," Murphy replied, rising and making for the door. Dunning wobbled after him, the cold, humid Irish night striking him like a slap in the face.

"I'll be doing the driving," Gilchrist shouted in his ear, thrusting the publisher into the passenger seat. Dunning let him assume command and drive like a lunatic. If we hit a mine, we won't have time to blow up at this speed, Dunning was reflecting as he fell asleep. He woke up at the Nelson Hotel, where his companion snatched the key off the hook and pulled him upstairs and into his room. "Now, we can look at the contracts," he said, locking the door.

Sitting on the bed, Dunning observed with bleary eyes

how this man sat at the table to scan the printed contract carefully; again and again, he studied the lines of each clause dealing with the advance money, royalties and various rights. Finally, he turned to Dunning and said sharply, "I cannot be putting my name on this. I am asking at least two thousand pounds' advance and royalties of fifteen percent on sales of over four thousand copies, and I want eighty percent of the serial and translation rights."

"I'll have to speak to London about that," Dunning mumbled. "Have you read those clauses guaranteeing your friend, Faulds, isn't an IRA member or a criminal? If you sign those and anybody proves he's one or the other, the contract becomes null and void."

"I can give my word Faulds is neither an IRA gunman nor a criminal." Gilchrist threw both copies of the contract back at Dunning. "When you've spoken to your bosses, let me know." He was heading for the door when Dunning called him back.

Dunning decided he could not face another ordeal like these last three days. It would kill him, literally. Perhaps he was too drunk to clinch a major deal, but something bellowed that he had to grab this will-o'-the-wisp Irishman now. For a book like *A Common Grave* what was a couple of thousand pounds? And the royalties this man was demanding were standard. "Look," he said, "if I alter the money clauses, will you sign the contract now?"

"Ay, that I will."

Dunning placed the two contracts on the bedside table; he could just about focus on the relevant clauses to make the changes, which he initialled before signing the bottom of each sheet. Murphy did the same with both contracts, keeping one copy. To Dunning, he handed a typed sheet on which he had noted the Swiss bank into which the money should be paid and through which all correspondence should be addressed.

Dunning had almost fallen asleep. Gilchrist slipped off

the publisher's shoes, lifted and swivelled his legs to lay him full-length on the bed. Covering him with a blanket, he put out the light. Outside the door, he listened to Dunning's snores before kissing his contract and dancing a little jig. Wait until he told Baldwin, and Anne, how easily he had pulled off the deal!

12

Baldwin realized he had written a winner by the haste to bring out *A Common Grave*. Normally, his publisher allowed anything from nine months to a year for editing, promotion and marketing; but they were halving this period and aiming at spring publication. Dunning flew to New York to negotiate a coproduction agreement and sold the book to Jensen and Reinhardt, the first American publishers who read it; they did not worry about Liam Faulds's anonymity or background; not did they haggle over the advance, paying $200,000 and generous royalties. Several film companies proposed buying options, but Baldwin advised waiting until after publication when they could ask ten times the option offer and pick a producer who could pay the right director and stars to make the film.

Gilchrist suggested shifting his undercover operation to London, but Baldwin vetoed this. When the book appeared, the Fleet Street press would discover he had a London base, flush him out and wreck their scheme. He would work in Ulster, insist on dealing only with Dunning, and even then keep the publisher at arm's length and guessing. Baldwin also warned the Gilchrists against spending too much of their $40,000 advance, which would alert people. Let the Swiss invest it and channel the interest through their London branches. Anne must keep her hospital job. He, Baldwin, would help her husband write several freelance pieces to put his name before the public and justify what he spent.

They ran no risks, making rendezvous in East End pubs and cafés to avoid recognition. Gilchrist amused them by mimicking Dunning's antics, and his fear of stopping an IRA bullet. "Know what?" he said. "He'd like me to get through to Faulds somehow and ask if he's got another book lined up. His firm's keen to have another Irish story to follow up *A Common Grave*." He gazed across the café table at Baldwin. "What do I do about that?"

"Tell him your contacts whisper Faulds is working on another book."

"Is he?" Anne queried.

"He's trying." In fact, Baldwin had envisaged a sequel to the first Faulds book. For weeks he had been dipping, vainly, into the notes and recollections of his nine months in Ulster, searching for a basic theme around which to develop characters and a plot. "String him along," he said.

Gilchrist had to return to Belfast to pick up final proofs of *A Common Grave*. He would be away from home for two or more weeks. "I hope you don't mind all these absences, Anne," Baldwin remarked when he was briefing Gilchrist.

"Mind! I'm only too glad to get him out of my feet for a day or two," she replied, then gave that full-throated laugh of hers.

Her husband had been gone three days when she called Baldwin. "Remember you read those stories of Martin's a couple of months or so ago?" she said. "I was having a look at them and noticed that on the one about the spastic child you'd written a comment. You said he'd be better to scrap the short story and turn it into a novel. Were you serious?"

"I couldn't have been more serious," Baldwin replied.

"There's not much call for short stories these days, and that one would make a first-rate novel. Why do you ask?"

"Oh, it was only I saw he'd had a go at scheming something like a long novel round the story idea," she explained. "But you know Martin well enough by now—he's always starting something, but somehow he never gets round to finishing it. I don't suppose he'll take this any further." She suddenly switched to telling him how Martin was faring in Northern Ireland, then chit-chatted for a few minutes before hanging up.

That call set Baldwin thinking. Anne Gilchrist had been referring to the story of their own tragedy, to the son they had loved and yet sacrificed, Michael, their mongol child. Of all Gilchrist's stories, only that one had impressed him. Straight away he had visualized it as a full-length novel, for no short story could ever have done justice to the personal drama of two parents torn between their own happiness and their love for a defective child. Both protagonists, the husband and wife, had to be drawn carefully; they had to reveal their deep motives and their real feelings and their characters had to evolve gradually. As the child's father, Martin Gilchrist had probably experienced a natural desire to write the trauma out of his system, but lacking the technical equipment, professional know-how or perhaps the intellectual stamina, he had come nowhere near achieving this. As he sat there in his study, remembering what Gilchrist had written, an idea flashed across his mind: Why not write the story himself with Anne and Martin Gilchrist prompting him with the facts? Just as quickly, he dismissed the notion, reasoning that Anne would never agree. Another objection struck him: he did not want to get too close to Anne Gilchrist. As well as being the wife of his collaborator and fellow plotter, she attracted him too much. All the same, as a Liam Faulds novel, he'd probably never find better. Would Anne wear it if he changed the names and placed the story in Faulds's territory, Ulster? The more he buffed the rough edges off the problem and examined its various facets, the more the story appealed.

And if he felt tempted to try seducing Anne Gilchrist, what prevented him from meeting her on neutral ground?

Two evenings later, he rang her. First, he probed delicately round the subject. Did Martin mean to identify himself or her by name or place in his projected novel? If he did, Baldwin could foresee a great many difficulties, not only personal ones for them when the book appeared, but with the Faulds business. Did Anne see any reason why he, Baldwin, should not write the story as a Liam Faulds novel, which might make as much money as *A Common Grave?* Faulds's publishers were pleading for a sequel and this seemed tailor-made.

At the outset, Anne bluntly rejected the idea; she demurred at the thought of supplying Baldwin with the intimate details of their married life, their quarrels, the trauma that their mentally deficient child had provoked. It was all too recent and had left them with wounds that had not yet scarred over. In any case, Martin was probably not attempting to write a serious book but merely unloading the memory of those years from his mind by transforming it to paper.

"But if it's done really well, it could be a book for both of you to be proud of," Baldwin insisted. And if he chose Ulster as the locale and changed the names, nobody could conceivably connect them with the story.

It took him a week of persuasive argument before Anne finally surrendered and consented to help him document the book. But she made several stipulations. They must do it together, without Martin's help. Without even his knowledge. "If you let on to him, he'll say no, point-blank, and I'll be forced to agree and there'll be no book," she explained. "You see, for him even more than me, it was something really sacred."

"But I don't know how we'll manage to keep it secret from him," Baldwin objected. "Anyway, at some time or other, he'll have to read the book."

"Oh, he'll be all right when it's a book and he reads it as such. He wouldn't be reliving the whole thing by helping you to write it, do you see?" Baldwin supposed he did, and nodded. "Anyway," she continued, "you're his idol and anything you do will find favor with him."

Without realizing or consciously wishing it, Baldwin had taken yet another step in his collusion with Anne Gilchrist. Later, he could discern how he had subconsciously tried to manoeuvre himself and her into such a situation. And Anne must have sensed this, too. A few days after agreeing to cooperate, he invited her to bring round Gilchrist's manuscript, or meet him somewhere with it, but she made an excuse and instead posted the story and the inchoate pages Gilchrist had scribbled in an effort to transform it into a novel. When Baldwin read this he realized the Ulsterman would never have succeeded in continuing the novel in his confessional style.

In reading the short story several times to ponder the scheme of a novel, Baldwin decided he would once again have to use the first-person narrative—as though he were the father of the mongoloid child.

However, when he came to revise the first chapter, he bogged down; after two days he was sitting in his study with drawn curtains, a full waste-paper basket and his umpteenth frustrated headache. For Baldwin, headaches spelled an attack of writer's block. If Baldwin feared one thing above all others, it was writer's block. He could not feel this novel and before he could do anything justice on paper he had to visualize or sense it. In desperation, on the third night of headaches, he phoned Anne. "I need help," he groaned. She listened, silently, while he exposed the problem. Without either herself or Gilchrist to orient him and prompt him with the right cues, he had no book. If she could spare him even an hour or two, he might untangle the writing problems. "I can see you any lunchtime," he suggested.

"No, I'll come by tomorrow night, after work."

"But your little girl, Moira?"

"I'll get a girl sitter from next door."

She arrived straight from the hospital, still clad in her

clinical white stockings, but wearing a pair of high-heeled shoes that set off her slender though strong legs; she wore no makeup or even nail varnish and her chestnut hair fell chaotically over her brow and shoulders. She looked tired. Baldwin handed her a whisky, urging her to sip it quietly before conducting her into his study; there, he switched on the tape recorder and encouraged her to tell her story. It surprised him, the flat, neutral accents with which she uttered the details, as though time had bleached the emotion and pain she had lived through and the words now connoted little or nothing. Baldwin filled in her elisions and blanks. He well imagined their apprehension when their child, Michael, seemed backwards compared with other children at the clinic they attended; then their shock and horror when paediatricians broke it to them piecemeal, sinister hints hardening into certainties. Their little boy had a chromosome abnormality and they must do tests. Anne had had no need to wait for those; over the weeks and months, she had noticed the failure to speak, the lack of limb and finger coordination, the mongoloid cast of Michael's features. Finally, the doctors confirmed their fears. Michael had Down's syndrome, an irreversible mental and physical deficiency; he would never speak properly, he would be incontinent and she would have to hand-feed him. Their world collapsed, crumbled. For weeks, both she and Martin sat at home, just looking at each other, saying nothing, wondering what had happened to their lives. Of course they quarrelled; about who was to blame for their abnormal son, which of them had carried those baleful rogue chromosomes and genes in his or her heredity; about how it would affect their careers and lives; about the money it would cost them when Anne had to leave her hospital job and look after Michael full-time; about the wear and tear on both of them; about the social stigma they'd have to bear with the child who stared desperately at them and who could do no more than whimper or cry like a stricken animal.

Anne was toying with a cigarette Baldwin had offered her before she lit it and drew the smoke deep into her lungs, releasing it with a sigh. "It sounds a bit callous, does·it?" she muttered. "And that's the way it was, if you want the truth?" She fixed him with her eyes, her mouth pinching into an expression of disgust. "In all those rows and heart-searching sessions, we'd both forgotten one thing—Michael. How did he feel? How would he live to enjoy whatever existence he had?" She smoked for a moment in silence, then went on. "Children like Michael may not be able to talk or act normally—but they have a sixth sense about whether they're wanted or not. Michael knew before we did ourselves that we were going to get rid of him."

"Why did you decide to put him into a home?"

"Oh, a lot happened before then," Anne replied. "We nearly split up, Martin and myself." Their bickering over the child and even his presence had driven a wedge between them and Anne began to suffer from depression. She reproached Gilchrist with not earning enough to hire someone to take over part of the burden of looking after Michael. Finally, she'd walked out on him, farmed the child out on her mother, in Belfast, and went back to her job. Anne fell silent, as though mentally playing back that phase of her story.

"But you finally made things up," Baldwin prompted.

She nodded. "Three months went by and Martin came to see me at the hospital. He coaxed me to give up work and bring the child back. He was earning a bit more money from his journalism. A few months after we made things up I found I was expecting another child."

"That must have worried you."

"It gave me the worst six months of my life wondering if it would be another boy like Michael. If it had been, I wouldn't have wanted to go on living." She ground out her cigarette. "I'd have thrown myself into the river, or put my head in the gas oven." She sounded as though she meant every word. When she looked at Baldwin he could see her eyes were hollow with weariness or the stress of relating her experience. "I've spouted enough for one night," she said.

"I'm sorry I've kept you at it all that time," Baldwin

said, switching off the tape recorder. Anne flopped back in her chair like a spring uncoiling. Baldwin excused himself for being so selfish and overlooking the fact she had toiled a long day in her hospital; he fetched them both whiskies. "Have you eaten anything?" he asked and she shook her head, saying she would boil herself an egg at home. Waving her objections aside, he went into the kitchen, heated a tin of lobster soup, and boiled two eggs; he apologized for not being able to buy her a decent restaurant meal, but they might be spotted. After he had set the table in the living room, he put his head round the study door to call her. She was standing gazing at the rows of his books in their various editions. For a moment or two he watched her running a blunt finger along the books as though caressing them; she extracted several to study their titles, shaking her head in wonderment at a Japanese edition and a Hindi translation. Suddenly noticing him, she started, flushed with guilt, then gestured at his wall of first editions and his portrait gallery. "You must feel pretty proud of all this," she commented.

"Of the first two or three," he said. "But nowadays I don't bother much, for I know what they'll signify in twenty or fifty years." He grinned. "I often feel conscience-stricken about adding to the hundreds of thousands of books on the shelves and murdering a forest of splendid trees to produce throwaway literature."

"Throwaway literature! A writer like you! You're not serious."

"Almost," he answered with a shrug. He held out a hand to lead her into the living room. She grasped it and he felt a slight pressure of her fingers and wondered if she were giving some sort of hint. They small-talked through the soup, but when they were eating the soft-boiled eggs with brown bread and butter, she glanced at him, askance, and said, "What was she like—your wife?"

"From the little I remember about her, she had a dogleg kink on the bridge of her nose, leftwards as you looked at her. I didn't notice it until we'd been married three weeks."

Anne laughed. "That's just a line of dialogue. I want the truth."

"All right. She was about half as beautiful as you."

"No, be serious," she insisted. "I've seen pictures of her and I know how pretty she was. But was she intelligent? Did she love you?"

He understood the drift of her questions and pondered for several moments before replying. "I suppose she must have loved me after her fashion. Or else she wouldn't have gone over me with paint-stripper, sandpapered my rough proletarian edges and done a complete recellulosing job on me."

Now Anne had puzzlement in her lambent brown eyes. "But that was because all women imagine their husbands in a certain way."

"And if they don't conform, they change them," Baldwin said. "And if they fail with the husband they get to work on the offspring to make sure they're moulded right." He noticed the pensive shifting of her eyes, as though she were thinking of the flawed child she could never have shaped according to her ideals.

"I saw the film of your play *Stalemate*. The gossip columnists said it was drawn from life."

"For once they were right," Baldwin said. "Full of home truths and home thoughts from abroad. But it gives a general idea of the in-fighting between me and my beloved." He refilled their wine glasses and offered her cheese and biscuits. "Half the trouble was Diana got me out of focus against the wrong background. I was an orphan boy, so she thought she could take me in hand and teach me everything—how to talk, how to clean the remaining fragments of Bermondsey accent and slang off my tongue, how to keep soup stains off my tie, and how to write my books."

"Who walked out on who?"

"She did—but well loaded with my best possessions, a fat settlement and lifetime alimony of nearly half my earnings." That thought angered him so much that he drove his ex-wife out of his mind. He raised his wine glass to Anne and smiled. "Enough of my past mistakes. Let's drink to our future and *A Common Grave*."

"I'll drink to it," she agreed. "But I must confess I get so scared about it I sometimes have nightmares."

"Nightmares!"

"I dream they've discovered everything . . . Martin's done something daft and has been caught out . . . the press, TV, the whole country is after us. And we're all threatened with jail for tax fraud or false pretences or something worse. I'm always running down an endless hospital corridor with all the doors locked, and I always wind up in a dungeon with a barred window looking on to a firing squad and a Belfast priest giving me absolution. You know the sort of crazy dream that wakes you up trembling." She gazed at him. "Can anybody possibly find us out?"

"Not unless one of us cracks or slips up," Baldwin replied. Patiently, he recapitulated all the steps he had taken, detailing the plan they had agreed on and the precautions against its discovery. Still she seemed dubious.

"Nobody could find the manuscripts—the original ones you wrote and copied," she suggested.

He shook his head. "They're safely in my bank vault along with the copy of the document we signed with the lawyer."

"Of course, that document," she mused. "Ours is lying in a tin box with the insurance papers and our birth certificates. I must get Martin to do the same as you—pay for a bank strongbox and keep it there." Her gaze seemed far away as he poured them coffee and liqueurs, but she retrieved the subject. "There's a third document, isn't there—with your lawyer. But he'd never let us down, would he?"

Baldwin laughed. "You've met him yourself and I can vouch for him all the way. Anthony Lewis is fireproof."

"It was probably a stupid notion," she said, "but I started thinking he might blackmail us or let some third person in on the secret. After all, there's a lot of money involved in the Faulds book."

Baldwin stifled his amusement, remembering what Lewis himself had said about the possibility of being blackmailed by the Gilchrists. "It's a case of all hanging together," he said, grinning, but he noticed she did not respond to his good humor. "No, I'm joking," he said. "I trust Lewis. He's a bachelor, so he doesn't have a wife to confide in, and the paper's safe in his own home with nobody else in the know." He reached over to clasp her hand and squeeze it. "So, you can stop having those nightmares. If we all keep our mouths shut and Martin keeps his nose clean, nobody can find out until we're good and ready to tell them."

"When will that be?"

"When we're all millionaires and we've sucked the orange dry and the hunt for Liam Faulds has run out of steam and he needs resuscitation."

She appeared satisfied with his reassurance and started talking about his books. She knew his novels and plays almost as well as he did and he marvelled at how shrewdly she had analyzed his persona; she had guessed rightly his literary output was a projection or a reflection of his own nature and personality. Bit by bit, she manoeuvred him into telling his story. "Tit for tat," she laughed. Flattered by her interest, Baldwin described his orphanage days, his beginnings as a writer and some of the important assignments he had carried out for national newspapers. She gazed, wistfully, at him. "It must have been hard, feeling absolutely alone in the world," she murmured.

Baldwin nodded assent. "There are still things I yearn to know and shall never know. Who my parents were and where they were from, the sort of earth they sprang from and can return to." He looked at her. "Even the dead like company," he said.

"You haven't many friends," she remarked, and he shook his head. His real foster parents, David and Elizabeth Graham, had gone back to New Zealand to farm and he did not trust friends he had made since the fame that had followed *Not in the Script*.

She left just before midnight. He accompanied her to his car, which he kept in a parking bay a hundred yards from his flat, then drove her to Fulham Road. In case a neighbor might be watching, he dropped her well away from Simon Close. She promised him several hours the following week to continue taping her story, just before Gilchrist flew back from Northern Ireland; by then he reckoned to have written a couple of chapters of the first draft for her to read and perhaps copy.

"I suppose Martin will have to be in Ulster when *A Common Grave* is published," she whispered as they sat in the car.

"I'm afraid so," he replied. "Dunning will probably have dozens of queries and offers when the book appears and he'll want to contact Martin."

"I wonder how it will do."

"We'll soon find out. Dunning let slip the other day they're publishing at the end of next month and they've lined up a big press, radio and TV campaign to launch the book."

13

Whenever Baldwin switched on his car radio or TV set, it seemed the name Liam Faulds leapt out at him. It confronted him everywhere in piled volumes in the bookshops, on hoardings and bus ads, in newspapers and magazines. Wherever he went, people appeared to be discussing *A Common Grave* and its enigmatic author. Some thought it brilliant, others maudlin and melodramatic; several critics praised it as a peace parable, with love reuniting the warring Irish factions, while a cynical few pointed to the place where all Protestant and Catholic sectarian feuding seemed to end— the grave. Liam Faulds also split the critics and commentators. For some, the mystery surrounding him amounted to no more than a stunt by some well-known author with the collusion of his publisher, although the majority plumped for the theory that Faulds was a criminal on the run, or an IRA member who had fallen foul of his organisation. Aware that controversy was the life-blood of literature, Baldwin revelled in these arguments. He was also discovering hidden aspects of his own book, political and emotional overtones that he could only impute to his subconscious, but, after all, the inner mind he felt to be the well-spring of all real artistic creation. On the marketing side, the book ran away. So much so that Gresham and Holt could hardly keep pace with the reprints. Newspapers reported that Associated Artists had bid a small fortune for the film rights, and the paperback rights in Britain and America fetched an advance of £200,000, twice as much as any of his other books. All told, *A Common Grave* had earned nearly £400,000 within weeks of publication and Baldwin computed that it might rake in half as much again when fully exploited.

Even Dunning's acidulated features showed some spark of vitality when Baldwin met him for lunch a couple of weeks after the book had appeared. "But what a pother, ol' fellow," he moaned. "I've got press, TV, radio, magazines, the lot round my neck all wanting to know who the devil Liam Faulds is." Sucking in several drops of wine, he rolled them carefully round his tongue and mouth before committing them to his alimentary system. "And if I as much as whisper to anybody even the identity of his front man, Murphy, that would be the end of Faulds and *A Common Grave* as far as we're concerned."

"Does it matter? He's a one-book man, isn't he?"

Dunning held up both hands with two fingers crossed.

"You mean, he's got another book on the stocks?" Baldwin queried.

"It's all very hush-hush, so mum's the word, but he's working on something from what I can glean," Dunning whispered. "I hope we get the manuscript before he wins the Eddystone Prize for his first novel."

"You've already given him that, then."

"Who else is there?" Dunning sniffed. With a rare flash of cynical wit, he added, "We won't even have to rig the jury for him. The public will have done that."

"But won't you have to flush Faulds out of hiding to receive the Eddystone?"

"Not if we can help it," Dunning affirmed. "After all, they've given the Nobel *in absentia*." Showing a certain verve mixed with sour humour, he went on to describe his ordeals in Ulster; how Murphy, the front man, had him chasing all over Northern Ireland—yes, and once into the Irish Republic—to keep appointments among dens of IRA thugs, smugglers, gun-runners, poteen distillers and God-knew-what.

"This Murphy—what's he like?"

"A real bandit," Dunning replied with feeling. "A great hulking, black-bearded scoundrel with a face like Brian Boru, a mind like Machiavelli and a thirst like a whole caravan of camels." Dunning's voice vibrated with distaste as he continued. "You can almost smell the blood and gunpowder on his hands."

"Have you thought how good it'll look if some IRA defector or informer suddenly takes it into his head to reveal Liam Faulds is one of theirs still," Baldwin said, rubbing grit into Dunning's eyes.

"On that day, I make for the Snowy Mountains," Dunning said with another flash of acid wit. "I've an Australian cousin who raises eucalyptus trees and has a spare shack for me."

"I'll miss you, Keith," Baldwin said pointedly.

That night, Baldwin invited Gilchrist to his flat after dark to pass on what he had gathered from Dunning about the various deals he was setting up with paperback firms, foreign publishers, film companies. He sent Gilchrist home to pack his bags and props and fly to Belfast, ready to receive any phone calls from Dunning and fix meetings with him. Baldwin hammered into the young Ulsterman that from now on things would become really tricky for all of them since Fleet Street and the world press would start a serious hunt for Liam Faulds, hoping he would turn out to be an IRA gunman and they could print his real story and work up a scandal round the book. They were already badgering Dunning and would try to follow him on his Irish trips, so Gilchrist might have to arrange to sign contracts without physically meeting the publisher; he might have to conduct negotiations with him by phone and pick up any documents through a post-box in one of the post offices; or better still, copy the undercover agents' technique and use a hole in the wall or that type of prearranged dead-drop. When retrieving letters, he must use his various disguises.

"How long do you think this hunt will last?" Gilchrist asked.

Baldwin shrugged. "Three weeks—probably a month at the most. But some newspaperman might see it as a challenge and keep looking, so watch out for booby traps."

"From what I've seen, Dunning might crack."

"That's why you've got to keep him at arm's length."

"What do I say about the next book?"

"Stall him. Tell him three or four months."

Baldwin had, in fact, completed the first three chapters of the book, toiling over them more slowly and deliberately than he had ever done. He had given no more than the first three chapters to Anne to copy for he had not seen her during the month Gilchrist had been living in London, so scared was she that he might discover their collaboration. Baldwin chafed to resume work on the book. Or so he assured himself. He also had to admit that he wanted a motive for meeting Anne Gilchrist again, for he had missed her. Perhaps that accounted for his guilt feelings when he drove Gilchrist to London Airport and dropped him near the British Airways terminal. When he returned that evening, he phoned Anne and asked if they might see each other. Was he deluding himself, or did she seem as eager to come over? Anyway, she agreed to meet him the following evening.

Baldwin went out and did his own shopping, stinting nothing. He acquired several expensive bottles of Chambertin, two of the more expensive Château d'Yquem because she liked its sweetish taste, a large tin of caviar and *foie gras*. In Harrods he bought a shoulder of lamb, boned and rolled and seasoned the way she liked it; he loaded up with vegetables and chose her favorite cheeses, Brillat Savarin, Roquefort, Époisse. Back in his flat, he spent the two hours before her arrival cooking. When Anne arrived, she gazed at the table, marvelling. She was wearing a new dress with a high neck, flap sleeves and new Italian shoes. She had also added a touch of rouge to her high cheekbones and heightened the brown of her eyes with a smear of silver eye-shadow. "What's all this for?" she asked, indicating the banquet.

"Well, we've got a lot to celebrate and can't go out like ordinary rich people and live it up, so I thought we'd have a small fête right here." To emphasize his statement, he sent a champagne cork flying and poured them two glasses of the frothy liquor. Anne entered into the spirit of the thing, laughing whole-heartedly. Never before had she tasted caviar the way he said the Russians devoured it—bedded in thick butter on brown bread. When they reached the roast lamb, she pronounced it the best she had ever tasted. And the wines! They went over her throat like velvet. "But wherever did you learn to cook?" she asked, amazed.

"Living with my ex I had to or I'd have starved," he replied. "Even her toast invariably finished as charcoal. And since I'm not a social animal who wants to dine out every night of the week, I bought a stack of cookery books and learned the hard way." He caught her gazing at him with a new light in her eyes as if an intriguing thought were traversing her mind.

"I've never had a better meal at or away from home," she murmured when they had eaten cheese and fruit and were drinking coffee and liqueurs.

"You have to get used to a new living style," he said. "You're a wealthy woman, or didn't you know it?"

"I still can't believe it." She laughed. "I've always dreamed of having a barrowful of money, and the funny thing is now I have it, I can't spend it."

"Leave it a bit and we'll invent a rich American uncle who's made his fortune in oil, has no kin besides you, and he's willed you his wells."

"I wouldn't do that yet," she remarked, evidently taking him seriously.

"Why not?"

"Well, I worry about Martin sometimes," she said. "I hope all this money doesn't go to his head." She poured them more coffee and he refilled their liqueur glasses with kirsch. He waited for her to continue, watching the candlelight wavering over her strong features, creating the illusion she was trembling. "I often wonder if the pressure mightn't be too much for him."

"He's done brilliantly so far."

She toyed with her coffee spoon, then tossed her head. "You don't know him as well as I do. You know this story of ours you're writing—he's had at least twenty goes at it and every time he gives up. He hasn't added a line to it for months."

"Writers get mental block at times."

She laughed. "Martin must be a terminal case."

"Maybe I'm corrupting him with all this money."

"Oh, that's just one more excuse to add to the other hundred." She paused to stare into the candlelight, which made a flickering pinpoint in the pupils of her brown eyes. "Do you think he'll ever develop into a real writer?" she asked.

"But he can write," Baldwin retorted. "Those stories of his are proof."

Anne waved her cigarette in a gesture of dismissal. "You know yourself, the difference between his best short story and the way you're converting it into a novel is the difference between somebody playing the tin whistle against somebody playing an organ."

Baldwin shrugged, yet was flattered by the comparison. "Perhaps he doesn't have the sort of flair or mental kink that makes a novelist," he said. "But his talent will mature if he keeps at it."

"That answers my question," she murmured. "You know, I felt guilty about helping you with his and my story. I felt I might be betraying him." She shrugged, then as though she had taken a personal decision, she gulped the rest

111

of her coffee and liqueur and stood up, straight. "I suppose I'd better sing for my supper," she said. For a moment, Baldwin glanced at her, puzzled at what the idiom implied in this situation. Catching his perplexity, she said quickly, "I meant, aren't you going to switch on your recording machine and begin your interrogation?"

For a couple of hours they sat in his study while she continued her narrative of the transformation Michael, her mongol child, had wrought in her married life. From time to time, Baldwin's eye fell on the needle of the machine; it stayed steady because her voice hardly varied either in volume or in pitch. When finally he switched off the tape machine, she turned to him. "I suppose with your insight into human nature, you'll guess if I don't tell you, why Martin can't or won't write the story the way we lived it. He felt even more guilty than I did about putting ourselves before the child, that's why." It sounded so matter-of-fact, the way she uttered the comment.

Baldwin trailed after her into the living room, where she picked up her coat and put it on. Refusing his offer of a lift, she muttered that she needed air and time and solitude to think, so she would walk part of the way, then catch a bus. "Do you want to read these and copy them into your exercise books?" he asked, holding up the fourth and fifth chapters of the story. Anne nodded, accepted the folder without a word and left the house quickly. Baldwin sat down, perplexed by her sudden change of mood. Was she teasing him? At one moment, he thought she was inviting him to bed, then something happened and she reneged. Maybe she felt too guilty about taking the inevitable step—like him. Baldwin realized one thing; he wanted this woman more than any other he had ever loved.

For her part, Anne seemed more determined than himself to push ahead and finish the new book. When she next visited Baldwin at his flat, she carried not only the two latest chapters that she had copied but the bundle of exercise books she had filled up to date. She seemed perturbed and explained why. Only the other day, she had come across her child, Moira, playing with one of the books; it occurred to her that the baby-sitter might stumble on them in their hiding place, read them and thus jeopardize everything. And what happened if Martin suddenly landed, unannounced, from Ireland and discovered the novel in its unfinished form? He would conclude they were stabbing him in the back— and not only by writing his story in secret. "I must have somewhere else to keep these copies," she said. "In fact, I don't feel safe even copying the material in my flat."

"No problem," Baldwin said. "Why don't you come here in your spare time and copy what I've done? You can use the study when I'm not here, and the living room if I happen to be working."

After some hesitation, Anne acquiesced, saying she might use the flat two or three nights a week. Baldwin presented her with a set of keys for the front door and his study cupboard and showed her how the flat ran. If she felt hungry, she could raid the fridge and make herself lunch or dinner. Although he trusted the Taylors, he advised Anne not to work in the flat while Ina Taylor was cleaning, which she normally did during the forenoon.

Baldwin was spending mornings and part of his afternoons on the Gilchrists' story. However, from the turn of the year, he had been receiving books proposed for the Eddystone Prize and some of these he had to read carefully and report on to the foundation secretary. He also had to keep contact with Dunning and other friends in Gresham and Holt to learn how Liam Faulds and *A Common Grave* were progressing. When he shut up his study he left what he had written and revised in the locked cupboard for Anne to copy when she arrived from the hospital on her two or three evenings a week. Sometimes, either he or she cooked a meal and they ate it together, but often, too weary after her day's work and two hours' copying, she had him drive her home. Outside their working routine, they rarely discussed the novel, but on one occasion, several weeks after their new arrangement, Anne turned to him. "Graeme," she murmured, "you know more about me than even my confessor, or my husband." She made it sound like a quip, but her tone did not deceive him. For it was true. With the amount of cross-examining and probing he had done for the book, he had gained more insights into this young woman's nature and personality in a matter of weeks than he had ever touched after years with Diana. He never asked her, but frequently wondered what Anne thought of the pages he had composed about her married life with Gilchrist. Since he was writing from the husband's viewpoint, he had tried to imagine himself as Gilchrist falling in love with this lovely and strong-willed woman. Baldwin had to draw Anne's literary portrait and he realized that nothing flattered a person as much as watching her own portrait emerge under the hand of a painter, writer or any other artist, regardless of flaws or lop-sided judgments. Yet, Anne Gilchrist hardly ever uttered any comment on those pages that she was transforming from his typescript into her bold, ornate longhand in the exercise books.

However, one evening he arrived home and went into the study to find her crying by the window. Her school jotter lay open. He noticed she had reached that point in the narrative where she and her husband had decided after much heart-searching and wrangling to place Michael in a home for backward children. "Anne, what's the matter?" Baldwin said, approaching and putting his arm around her.

"Nothing . . . nothing . . . just that it's all so true . . . so true." She was sobbing. "I never thought I'd cry about it again . . . never. I thought I'd cried myself dry."

"I'm sorry," Baldwin muttered. "I didn't mean to hurt you with what I wrote."

"Hurt me!" she repeated. "No, you haven't done that. What you've written is so beautiful and so true that I can see my son as he was. I can see bits of him I missed when he was with me. And I can relive all those moments with him. And

I can regret . . . which is what I should do." Blindly, she grasped the handkerchief he offered, wiped her eyes and cheeks, then blew into it. "I feel just as guilty, but . . . well, I don't know if you'll understand this . . . I feel he's not dead if he's there in those pages and in my mind and other people's."

"I understand how you feel."

"How did you do it? How did you know we both felt the way we did?"

"I don't know—a bit of intuition and a bit of guess-work," he replied. Should he confess? After deliberating for several moments, he said finally, "Perhaps I shouldn't tell you this, but I imagined myself as Martin."

Anne raised her head to stare at him as if she had suddenly discovered the solution of something that had baffled her. She shook her head, incredulously. "But Martin never said anything as beautiful as your words to me. I don't even remember him ever using the word love. And yet you made him say it to me so many times as though he meant it."

Baldwin smiled at her. "I couldn't imagine anybody who knew you being able to stop himself from saying he loved you—especially your husband."

Anne turned her face away from him to stare through the window towards the garden. She spoke in a musing voice. "You know, when something like Michael happens, it strikes at the true character of people—your parents, relatives, even your best friends. It sorts out the real people from the fake ones in the way I would imagine an air raid sorts them out." She started to cry once again and Baldwin tightened his arm round her to comfort her. "It sorted us out," she said. "It took Michael and everything that went with him to make me realize that Martin didn't love me. And I discovered it just when I needed him most . . . when our families were quarrelling and we had hardly any money and hardly any friends left."

Baldwin pulled her close to him, feeling the heaving of her breast and even sensing the strong, rapid heart pulse.

"Anne, don't cry," he whispered. "Come on, I'll build you a stiff drink." She shook her head but followed him into the living room, where she sat down, mumbling that she had a headache. He threw three aspirin tablets into a glass, squirted some soda water into it to dissolve them and offered her this. She drank the mixture. "Why don't you lie down for a couple of hours, then I'll run you home?" he suggested. She nodded and he led her into the bedroom where he turned down the bed cover, closed the curtains and left her there.

In his study, he worked for a couple of hours but without much concentration. So she did not love Gilchrist, nor did he love her. Baldwin tried to decipher what she had revealed in that conversation. She had spoken as though she really despised Gilchrist for his weakness, his lack of talent or will—yes, and even virility. As for himself, Baldwin had imagined he was acting out the part of Gilchrist in the story when he had merely been playing himself. And Anne had guessed or sensed this; she had read between the lines of what he had written in the novel and realized how he felt. Had he fallen in love with her truly? Or did he merely love the creation he had put on paper? Puzzling over that for several minutes, he decided he might never know the answer.

An hour later, when he edged the bedroom door open to ask how she was, she called, "Come in, Graeme—I'm all right." He moved, quietly, over to her bedside. She said, "Sorry I went to pieces like that."

"Blame me for choosing that story and touching on raw nerves and emotional wounds that haven't healed," he retorted. "If you like, we can scrap this book and come up with another idea."

"No—never!" Her voice rang surprisingly strong in the small bedroom. She stretched out a hand to grasp his; her hand felt warm, even feverish. "You didn't understand what I was trying to say, then?" He shook his head. She tugged on his hand and arm, then drew his head down, close to her face, and whispered. "I was trying to say I've fallen in love with you."

"Anne, isn't it the story you've fallen in love with?"

"No, it was happening before we started writing the story," she said. "Long before." Pulling his face down on hers, she kissed him. "It's you I love," she whispered, fondling his face, reconnoitring each feature with her hands, then suddenly crushing him against her body. Never had he known any woman embrace him with such force. In a moment, their bodies were tangling. He stripped off his clothes, kicking them away. She was undressing herself on the bed. He could feel her breath coming in short, sharp spurts as he explored her body, then entered her. Anne abandoned herself so completely that she seemed to him in some sort of trance during the sexual act, and for long minutes afterwards she appeared lost, disoriented. She behaved like some innocent, discovering the pleasure of love for the first time. As he lay beside her, Baldwin wondered what sort of lover Gilchrist had ever been to her.

For some time they lay together without speaking. When they rose and dressed, she came over to kiss him, then hug him. They had entered into an entirely new relationship, as lovers. They had started as allies in one plot, then as collaborators in a plot within that plot to deceive Gilchrist with their new book; from there, they had taken the final step and were betraying him and had begun their real complicity. However, as Baldwin drove to Fulham, he experienced no remorse about making love to Anne Gilchrist. He only worried and wondered about what a strong-willed and emotional woman like this one, who had her head cradled on his shoulder, might expect after confessing her love and giving herself to him.

14

In the *Sunday Herald* office, Harvey Quayle was leafing through a pile of newspapers, trying to unearth a follow-up story for the next edition, when his buzzer went. His editor's gravelly whisper summoned him to his room—dubbed the arena because it was round. A lot of bull-baiting went on there and many newspapermen had tottered out of it having received the *estocada* and looking as if the sword were still quivering between their shoulder blades. When Quayle entered, his editor, Jack Gibbon, picked up a sheaf of newspaper cuttings, flourishing them like a fly-whisk. "What are your thoughts on the Liam Faulds story?" he asked.

"I thought it had died a natural."

"Well, it hasn't and we're going to knock the scab off it or my nose is letting me down."

"I haven't even read the book," Quayle protested. When Gibbon got a hunch, somebody had to match it with the right story or receive the *estocada*.

"I haven't read that crap either," Gibbon grated. "I'm no literary buff and I'm not interested in an Irish Romeo and Juliet—only in the man that's supposed to have written it."

One of the most scabrous tongues in Fleet Street, Gibbon was tiny but had an outsize head. A dent in his right cheekbone from a car accident gave strangers the notion he was smiling. He never did. A small army of his Fleet Street throwouts had formed a Poison Dwarf Club in his honour, for mostly everyone over five feet five inches (Gibbon's height) got a quick *estocada*.

"It could make something if Faulds is on the run or belongs to the IRA and is paying his book proceeds into the munitions fund," Quayle remarked.

Gibbon pointed two saffron fingers and his glowing cigarette at his journalist. "Maybe there's something in the man-on-the-run theory," he rasped. "But that IRA yarn!" He shook his snow-white mane, disseminating dandruff like cigarette ash. "There's no propaganda percentage in his book. And if the IRA needed money, they'd rob a couple of banks or put the hat round Boston and New York and earn fifty times more than a dozen sob stories."

"It's a hoax, then."

"That would make just as good a yarn."

"Why our sudden interest?" Quayle asked.

"This hit my desk this morning." Gibbon flicked a typewritten note to Quayle. It was in block letters and read:

YOU SHOULD KNOW KEITH DUNNING OF GRESHAM AND HOLT IS MEETING LIAM FAULDS IN BELFAST NEXT FRIDAY. DUNNING WILL STAY AT THE EUROPA HOTEL. FAULDS CHANGES HIS HOTEL FOR EACH VISIT AND ALSO USES DIFFERENT NAMES. HE HAS STAYED AT THE GLENTORAN AS MURPHY. HE HAS MET DUNNING AT THE NELSON HOTEL IN STRABANE AND THE SION ARMS PUB NEAR THE BORDER. FAULDS IS BIG WITH BLOND HAIR AND BEARD AND CULTURED ULSTER ACCENT. A SOLICITOR CALLED RYAN IN DUBLIN ALSO KNOWS ABOUT LIAM FAULDS.

"No signature."

119

"Some of our greatest literature is anonymous," Gibbon replied.

"If it's true, this tip-off is worth a lot of money. Who would pass up good money?"

"Somebody who has it in for the publisher, or this man Faulds." Gibbon lit another cigarette from his glowing stub. "Anyway, you're wasting time."

"How much can I spend?" Quayle asked.

Gibbon studied the sad-sack face. Quayle was a mercenary, but one of the best investigative reporters in Fleet Street. "We won't query your expenses if they're not too dishonest," he replied. He thrust his pile of cuttings across the desk. "I've shoved in the half-dozen articles written by Graeme Baldwin, the novelist, on the Ulster troubles and the IRA. There's a couple of stories could put you on the track of the families mentioned by Faulds. Baldwin's a difficult bastard, prickly, and he's going through a meteor shower at the moment. I'll ring and ask if he'll see you."

"No, Jack," Quayle said. He never liked interviewing people cold, only after he had armed himself with the facts and could fire the sort of questions that panicked people. He walked out with an expenses chit for a hundred pounds and left the *Herald* office to stroll up the street to Mooney's Irish House. There, he filtered into company with Frank Leary of the *Irish Telegraph* and two journalists from the *Irish Independent* and *Irish Press*. Tossed into this circle, the name Liam Faulds set the talk frothing like the heads on their Guinness glasses.

Soon, Quayle gleaned where Dunning had stayed on various Ulster trips to meet Faulds. Leary had traced him to Rathlin Island, and one of the other men to Strabane; they mentioned half a dozen IRA haunts in Belfast and the name of a local treasurer for the IRA; but nobody had ever clapped eyes on Faulds. "Whoever he's after being, this Faulds is as sharp as a fiddler's bitch," Leary said. "What I'd be after knowin' is where's he hiding all that money."

Money. There's the key to the mystery, Quayle told himself as he left the Irish drinking school. In his book, two things dictated human conduct: money representing power and pleasure; and sex, representing lust or, as the mugs would say, love. He wandered back to his desk in the *Herald* office and, as he lunched off a sandwich and a mug of canteen tea, he studied the cuttings and that morning's notes. All that newsprint mileage on Liam Faulds, and nobody had a single clue about him. Well, he would start by scaring the hell out of Keith Dunning. Threading paper and carbon copies into his machine, he started to type quickly, knowing this story would never appear:

Belfast, Saturday
How many guns and grenades, how much ammunition does a quarter of a million pounds buy? How much gelignite? How many IRA murderers will such a sum of money recruit and train?

Let's say enough to kill a few hundred innocent civilians, Ulster policemen and British soldiers. Enough to light yet another powder barrel under the already erupting Ulster situation. Enough to trigger a real civil war.

Don't imagine this quarter of a million pounds comes from Irish-American sympathisers in the United States or from IRA bank and post-office robberies. No, it comes from a highly respectable source in Britain via a numbered Swiss bank account concealing the name of Mr. Liam Faulds. A name known to the millions of readers who have bought his book, *A Common Grave*.

These days, the IRA has some curious paymasters. Among them, Gresham and Holt, who publish Mr. Faulds as well as the Bible, the Book of Common Prayer and other religious works. But those paymasters include everyone who has unsuspectingly invested in a copy of the Faulds book, which means public libraries spending public money.

For Liam Faulds is a cover name for someone who channels the money into IRA funds to pay its killers, their guns and bombs. How do I know? It is common talk in any one of half a dozen IRA pubs and meeting places that I have visited here. Also, I have verified it with a top IRA man, Mr. Con O'Cassidy, treasurer of the Belfast Provo Brigade.

121

When the IRA choose to reveal the part they have played in the Faulds farce, Gresham and Holt will have to answer some awkward questions about how they allowed themselves to be duped into becoming major contributors to IRA funds and thus to bombing and bloodshed in Ulster.

I spoke to the editorial director of Gresham and Holt, Mr. Keith Dunning. He conducted the secret negotiations with Faulds and has met him in various rendezvous in Ulster including the Sion Arms, near Strabane, and the Nelson Hotel in Strabane. Mr. Dunning's next meeting with Faulds takes place in Belfast next Friday. Dunning admits he has no idea who Faulds really is. He cannot prove his author is not an IRA member. He also refuses to name the amounts he has paid into Faulds's Swiss bank.

Arriving at Gresham and Holt's office, Quayle sent his card and a note to Dunning, explaining his visit and requesting an interview. A middle-aged woman emerged from the lift, smiling. "I'm afraid Mr. Dunning's very busy and cannot see you. Perhaps you could write." Quayle handed her a copy of his story. "Give him this and tell him we go to press in a few hours with the page it will appear on. Ask if he's got any comments." Quayle picked up the Gresham and Holt catalogue, which told him the Faulds book had run through a dozen reprints and had sold two million hardback and paperback copies in Britain and America and had gone into fifteen foreign languages. Dunning's secretary returned, begging him to follow her.

Dunning was standing in his office, looking like an enraged rabbit. As though warding off the evil eye, he was holding Quayle's story at arm's length. "But this is absolutely monstrous," he shouted.

"I couldn't agree with you more," Quayle murmured, blandly misinterpreting the statement. "And I think the public will agree when it appears."

"I mean it's monstrous because it isn't true." Dunning got out. "Why, you even affirm here you've spoken to me."

"Well, I have, haven't I?" Quayle said. "And if what

I've written isn't true, you have the chance to put me right before we print the story."

"I see your little game," Dunning exclaimed. "You want me to endorse what you've written, or commit myself verbally. Well, it's failed." He tossed the two sheets across his desk. "Go ahead, print this rubbish—but you may have to prove these statements in the law courts."

"That would mean you'd have to produce Liam Faulds, or admit you don't know who he is."

Dunning glared at the pallid weasel face. He had no doubt this smooth-talking Grub Street homunculus would print this *canard*, which would provoke a rash of similar stories until Gresham and Holt had to sue for libel; he, Dunning, would have to admit on oath he had never met Faulds, only his proxy, another mystery man calling himself Murphy. Furthermore, he could predict the effect of such publicity on the firm's sales graph, its credibility and the apocalyptic temper of Hanbury-Giles. He would never survive the disgrace. Just his luck when the Faulds hunt had died down and they had the Eddystone Prize in their pockets. If he had always anticipated someone was going to flush Faulds out and reveal the truth, he had envisaged this happening under his control. Not slung at everybody in bludgeoning headlines by a maverick journalist. "How did you know I was going to Belfast on Friday?" he asked.

"Someone who knows Liam Faulds tipped us off."

"I lend that no credence whatever," Dunning said, but dubiously.

Realizing he had scared the publisher, Quayle began to ram home the facts in the anonymous note, giving Faulds's description and how they had first established contact through Ryan, the Dublin solicitor; he hinted Faulds had been spotted in various IRA haunts. "It's a dangerous game you're playing, Mr. Dunning," he said.

"What does that imply?"

"Let's say the IRA are behind this whole stunt and are buying guns with your story. If those hard men decide they cannot trust you not to talk about your contacts, they will shut you up for good." Quayle let his sinister remarks strike home before going on. "It's very easy to invent quotes. People know I've seen you. It would be your word against mine, and you can't sue. Anybody reading the *Herald* would think you'd talked too much. And they'd be waiting for you when you meet Faulds on Friday."

Fear walked up and down Dunning's back. How had this little newshound amassed so many details? More than enough to ruin everything if he printed them. Now the little rat was blackmailing him. Yet, his assertions about the IRA had already occurred to Dunning. He might easily be playing with his life. "What do you really want from me, Mr. Quayle?"

"Just to be behind you next Friday to help you find out who Mr. Faulds really is." Quayle raised a hand as though oath-taking. "Don't worry, nobody will see me."

"I'll think about it."

"No time," Quayle said. "In four hours this story goes into type. And every time you make a trip to Ulster or anywhere else, I'll be behind you and I shall run Faulds down or prove he doesn't exist, except as an IRA front man. And on that day, I wouldn't like to be you."

"You're proposing I collaborate with you?"

"All you have to do is drop the odd hint."

"All right," Dunning conceded after some hesitation. However, he made Quayle promise to publish nothing before they had both agreed on the date and content of the story. Faulds's representative, the man he knew as Murphy, had informed him that Faulds was working on the final chapters of another book and he did not want to compromise the signing of a contract for this novel. For his agreement, Quayle exacted photocopies from the publisher of one of the exercise books Liam Faulds had used to record the story of *A Common Grave*.

15

Anne had her head bent over the exercise book into which she was copying from his typescript when Baldwin entered the flat. Tiptoeing into the study, he stood observing her, noting how the circle of amber light from his desk lamp highlighted her tawny hair, and how her practical hand moved regularly across the page with that curious handwriting, full of loops and hooks and whorls. So immersed did she seem in his script that only when he tossed his key-ring onto the blotter did she raise her head; she had that same faraway expression people often perceived in his face when his mind had gone elsewhere and something pulled him back to the present. Pointing to the three completed exercise books, he murmured with astonishment, "Have you done all that this evening?" Anne nodded, then said, "Once I'd started I couldn't go fast enough to read what you'd written."

"But it's too much!" he exclaimed. "You're killing yourself, and you know there's no hurry for this book."

"How can you talk when you've been writing and revising a whole long chapter every week?" she said. "I know it's different—you're creating and I'm only copying and I can do that any time. But I'm still dying to see how it finishes."

"I don't know myself yet," he confessed. "But I would say I've no more than ten, twenty pages to write." While speaking, he reached over and tugged the cheap ballpoint pen from her hand, flipped the typewritten pages shut, then picked up the exercise books. These he placed in the cupboard with the remainder of the typescript and copied text. He locked the door and pocketed the key. "Never confuse literature with life or living," he said with a grin, taking her hand and leading her into the living room. Now that statement he would never have uttered six months ago; then he would have said literature for him *was* life and living. Moreover, he would have buckled down to his machine at this stage and wrestled with the end of the book under the illusion that he was shaping both his characters' destinies—and his own.

"How're you going to end it?"

"As the words arrange themselves in my head and on paper," he replied, half tongue-in-cheek.

"It staggers me how quickly you've done it," she said.

"But you made it easy," he answered. Catching the look of interrogation in her eyes, he added, "Oh, I don't mean because you put a lot of it on tape, or because I was drawing from a live model. I mean, you managed to make me live your story with you. So, it's your book in a sense."

"That's rubbish and you know it," she countered. "That book could never have been written by Martin if he'd spent twenty years on it—and he lived the story."

Baldwin could not argue against the truth. For the first pages of the book, he had attempted to place himself in Gilchrist's skin, though what he had, in fact, done was to imagine himself as Anne's lover. And for anyone who knew the relationship between Anne and Gilchrist, or between Anne and himself, this must have shown through in the text. After all, he had felt that love. In those four months he had spent writing this book, he could have climbed Everest, then

126

swum the Channel; he experienced that exhilaration of body and mind that swamped him when a book seemed to be creating itself and all he had to do was stand, like some ringmaster flicking his whip to bring on the various personalities, watch them perform their acts and prompt them every now and again with a word or a gesture. Not once did he have an attack of his old phobia about writer's block. Only one thing had niggled: How would Anne react when he had to describe Michael's death in the mental home and the emotional storm that gripped her and Gilchrist? To his amazement, she had taken even that calmly. No remorse, no hysterics, no Freudian catharsis.

Baldwin dared not admit it to himself, but in this book literature and life had somehow fused. And love. For though it took him months to acknowledge it, he had fallen in love with Anne Gilchrist. At the outset he had cheated, telling himself painters always fell in love with their models *after* they had painted them because, like every creator, they were enamoured of their own work. Well, he had tried to convince himself he was simply using Anne as a model and in writing those love scenes he had merely finished by believing them. But no, it was nothing like that. He had free-wheeled through this book as with no other because he was genuinely in love and that had transformed everything, even his writing and his style, even his sour philosophy. With *A Common Grave*, he'd had to toil and moil over the style; here, it came naturally. Had anyone handed him a Graeme Baldwin book and this second Faulds novel with no names on the covers, he would have sworn different authors, indeed differing types of individual, had spawned them. In revising the script, he sometimes did a double-take, wondering if he had actually created some of the narrative and scenes in this Faulds sequel.

"Have you found a title for it yet?" Anne asked, cutting across his reflections.

"I don't know," he replied. Titles always troubled him, and for several weeks he had been testing various phrases on himself as well as jotting down long strings of emotive words, injecting these into his mind and hoping for the right combination. "I wondered how this would strike you," he said. Tearing a leaf out of his notebook, he blocked in four words and passed the paper to her, considering the eye made more impact than the ear on the mind.

"'An Accident of Birth,'" she murmured, then repeated the phrase slowly, "'An Accident of Birth.'"

"Just think—would you buy something with that title?"

She hesitated, then nodded. "I'd look at it first and when I saw it was a novel . . . well, yes I'd buy it. Anyway, it's by Liam Faulds, isn't it?" She went to pour them both a Scotch and soda; he lit her cigarette and his own. Anne sipped the Scotch. "Yes, it's good, your title," she mused. "It sums up the book, and it's got bite."

"If you like it, that's what we'll call it," he said. "Now let's forget about the book. What has Ma Taylor laid in for us?"

"A choice between steak and frozen chips, or veal escallop, chips and beans. Or you have a chicken in the fridge."

"Chicken takes too long," Baldwin said, looking at his watch.

"Yes, but tonight we've all night, darling," Anne said. She laughed at the astonished lift of his eyebrows, then went on. "I lied in my teeth and said I was doing an emergency shift at the hospital, so Moira has gone to the neighbours for the night. And I've no hospital tomorrow. They owe me a day."

"But that's great," Baldwin said, hugging her. "A whole night ahead of us!" Anne had rarely spent the night in his flat because the neighbours might have spotted her and the gossip columnists would have descended on Baldwin asking awkward questions about the new girlfriend. She also had Moira to think of. However, she had farmed out the child for two weekends, which they had spent together in a small inn outside Thame in Oxfordshire. Baldwin kissed her. "It's too good to be true," he murmured, then crossed the room to pick up the phone and dial the Taylors' number, instructing his daily woman to forget her morning stint and make up for it the following day. He pleaded a rush job that would keep him busy all night. "In a sense, I suppose it's true." He grinned.

Finishing their drinks and cigarettes, they went into the kitchen to help each other prepare their meal. Baldwin seasoned and skewered the chicken while Anne prepared the vegetables and made a green salad.

"Liam Faulds won't last for ever," he commented as he picked a couple of cheeses from the fridge for their board and started to make fresh coffee.

Anne stopped chopping the herbs. "What do you mean by that?" she asked.

"Well, I suppose if somebody doesn't rumble Faulds, I'll finally be forced to put him into hibernation," he said. "I've still got Graeme Baldwin to think of and it'll look peculiar if I don't produce another book under my first pseudonym."

Anne resumed her chopping. She looked relieved. "For a moment I thought you were going to say we'd have to tell all," she said.

"One of these days we'll probably have to." Baldwin threw the next remark over his shoulder, casually. "But I suppose that'll depend on you and how you feel."

"Me! I've got nothing to do with Liam Faulds and you, except copy the book and play the message-boy between you and Martin."

"Yes, but if you were to stay here not just the odd night every other week, but well . . . if you were to move in with me for good . . ." Baldwin felt tongue-tied phrasing the suggestion. "You know what I'm getting at, Anne," he said finally.

Anne knew. Several times in the past weeks, he had broached the idea of a permanent relationship, but each time she had deflected him. When he had offered to push through a divorce from Gilchrist and marry her in a registry office to legalize their social situation she had pleaded that, as a practising Catholic, this would mean renouncing her religion. Her Irish family would break with her if she did that. Then there was Moira. Before taking any decision, she would have to discuss the girl's future with Gilchrist, who was still stuck in Ulster playing his cloak-and-dagger game with Dunning. Although they had separated once before—over their defective child, Michael—she did not know how Gilchrist would react to the suggestion of a permanent separation or a divorce. She contended she and Baldwin must wait until they had resolved some of their present problems and the Liam Faulds affair had finished.

"Are you worried about Gilchrist's share of the money?" he asked, and watched her brow furrow in thought. "If you are, I can assure you he'll be all right. He'll always collect the twenty percent on *A Common Grave* and this next book."

"Just give me time, Graeme darling," she begged. "A little more time." On a more cheerful note, she added, "Let's enjoy things while we can—as lovers." She put a possessive arm round him, looking at him wistfully. "When I was younger I used to think marriage was the biggest thing in life for me, but it didn't work out all that well, as you know."

"Maybe you're right," he said. "I didn't get much out of it, either. We're probably better to stay as lovers." By now, he had come to trust Anne's intuition and her good sense. Anyway, it was true that these stolen moments always tasted better and their complicity in the Faulds plot drew them even closer together and seemed to heighten their passion.

While they ate, he played their favourite records, nostalgic songs by Sinatra and Edith Piaf, a bit of jazz and rock music. Afterwards, they did something he had almost forgotten how to do—danced cheek-to-cheek and even intoned or hummed some of the melodies from his older records. With her head on his shoulder, her body pliant in his arms, Anne appeared as dreamy and sentimental as himself.

"Just think," she murmured in his ear, "we can lie as long as we want tomorrow."

"Sorry, sweetheart, not me," Baldwin said. "Didn't I

tell you I have to turn up at Shaftesbury Avenue at nine-thirty sharp for a meeting of the Eddystone Prize jury, and then sit through a lunch with that bunch of eunuchs? But you can sleep till noon and beyond if you feel like it."

"I might just do that," she said. "Then I can get on with copying *An Accident of Birth*."

"I can see I'll have to invent another Faulds story to keep you hanging on to me," he said, and she laughed in her old, free-and-easy way.

"Darling, you don't have to bribe me like that," she murmured.

Towards midnight she started clearing away the dishes and packing them into the washing-up machine. Watching her lithe, assured movements, Baldwin wondered about the fate that had thrust them together to play out their love in his flat, secretly. Their collaboration had deepened his feelings for her; in a curious way, he had shared the trauma she had suffered during those years with her defective son. For this, Anne Gilchrist meant more than the money or the prestige he might earn from the two books he had written under his *nom de guerre*, Liam Faulds. What Anne had got out of the arrangement he did not really know. Sometimes, in those funny brown eyes, he read doubt or distrust. Or was it fear? Yet, no one could dissimulate the passion she showed in love-making; and no one had ever evoked such ardour in him; Anne had restored not only much of his pride in his sexual prowess, but also repaired his ego, so badly mauled by contact with his frigid ex-wife, Diana.

He gave a hand to dry up the bits and pieces that did not fit into the dishwasher. "I can tidy the rest of the flat in my own time, tomorrow," Anne said, putting out the lights and making for the bedroom. Baldwin lay, watching her undress, appraising her lissome body and the lift of her breasts as she tied her long hair in a loose chignon. She slipped into bed and snuggled close to him. "Graeme darling," she whispered, "will you promise to remember always that I really love you?" She made him promise. And that night, she seemed to want to prove it to him time and again.

Baldwin woke just after eight. So that he would not disturb her, he grabbed his clothes, dressed in the living room and crept out of the flat to breakfast in a café in Church Street.

Anne slept until after ten, when she rose and made herself breakfast. After bathing and dressing, she tidied the flat, effacing every trace of herself from the bedroom, living room, kitchen and study so that neither Mrs. Taylor nor anybody else would know she had been there. By this time it had become a ritual to cover her tracks whenever she worked there on the book, even though the Taylors had been well coached by Baldwin in the art of discretion.

In the study, she started on the pages of typescript she had not copied, almost finishing them before lunch. She must badger and coax Baldwin to write those remaining pages quickly so that they had a complete book. After preparing and eating a snack lunch, she set to and did the rest of the script; she then rapped out a note to Baldwin saying she was now unemployed and would wait until he had fresh pages to copy before risking another visit to the flat. That should get him going again, she thought. With the keys he had given her, she opened the locked cupboard and placed her work and the note inside with the typescript, exercise books and the tape cassettes they had recorded earlier.

Beside these lay the gun. She had already noticed it many times, in its case behind the small deed box containing some of Baldwin's personal papers. Now, she could not resist lifting it out and studying the compact hand-grip and the squat barrel and the name, Beretta, engraved on it. There was also an extension piece she assumed to be a silencer. She pressed the clip release and realized that he kept the pistol loaded. To protect himself, he had affirmed when she had quizzed him about it. Anne wiped the pistol and replaced it in its box, then arranged everything as meticulously as Baldwin had left it. Thank God he had a tidy mind! Anne went through the writing desk, opening drawers and glancing at the diaries and papers. Baldwin, she knew, was compiling and editing his account of everything that happened in the Liam Faulds story and according to what he told her he would one day publish a book based on these diaries and papers.

Anne dusted the books. Baldwin's study had always fascinated her from the moment she had set eyes on those serried ranks of books in thirty-odd languages stretching the length and height of a whole wall; his portrait gallery with its celebrities on the opposite wall and the tools of his trade deployed on the big Chippendale desk also impressed her. She would have loved to be a writer, but realizing she lacked the talent, imagination and inspiration, she had done the next best thing and married Gilchrist, thinking he would become a famous author and she would walk in his aura. Disillusioned, she discovered he was a *fainéant* who could only blather about literature and at best fabricate a few nondescript articles for the sensational press. But Baldwin! He was a real writer who manipulated words and ideas that went like arrows to the heart or like heady wine or pep pills to the mind. Long ago, she had concluded that Martin could never have put the worst of Baldwin's books together had he lived to be two hundred.

She closed the drawers with a shrug. She had promised to tidy the flat and here she stood, daydreaming. Picking up her duster, she went over the books one by one, lovingly, then the desk and the furniture in the study. Baldwin smelled instinctively when anything had lost its place—a hangover from his orphanage days when he had so few possessions and cherished them all. By now, Anne knew where everything lived so well that she might have cleaned this study blindfolded. In mid-afternoon, when she had finished, she scrawled Baldwin another note, placing it in the locked drawer where he would be sure to find it. "Please, Graeme," she wrote. "Hurry up and finish it. I want so much to know what happens to me in those final pages. Yours with love. A."

16

Harvey Quayle caught the early morning Belfast flight on Friday, booking into a small hotel a mile from the city centre. From his room in the Europa, Dunning phoned later that morning to disclose that the front man, Murphy, had rung to discuss film option contracts the editor was carrying for his signature.

"Did you manage to fix a meeting with him?" Quayle asked.

"Wouldn't hear of it, ol' boy. As I said, we haven't met for months. He's too scared. He's had me use bombed houses, building sites, church collection boxes, drainpipes to plant his papers." Dunning went on lamenting, "It's no fun in Belfast, ol' man, trying to play undercover games with gunmen all around. Just try leaving a package anywhere and you wind up in a police station while they call the bomb squad."

"So, what's he decided now?"

"He'll let me know this evening."

To gather story background, Quayle walked through Belfast, an embattled city with its sandbagged buildings and police checkpoints, its blitzed ruins, its bleak housewives queueing to have their bags searched for bombs, weary of ten years' civil strife. A mile or two farther west, Quayle entered the real battleground between Catholics and Protestants, royalists and republicans, democrats and Marxists—the Falls Road and Shankill Road. Having now read *A Common Grave*, he needed no guidebook, since Faulds had used places like Divis Flats, Crumlin Road jail and Woodvale Park for powerful scenes. Faulds obviously knew this no-man's-land well, and its kids who were pelting police and army patrol cars with bricks and bottles, and the hostile faces peering from dilapidated terraced houses. No stranger and no Englishman lingered long in the Falls Road area, so Quayle retraced his way to the hotel where he found a message from Dunning.

On the phone, the publisher gave him the bad news. Murphy had again contacted him with precise instructions. Dunning would leave his hotel at nine o'clock the following morning carrying the film contracts wrapped in waterproof plastic bags; he would walk to the public lavatories at Callendar Street; he would place the wrapped contracts inside the cistern of number three toilet.

"Any idea when he intends to pick up these contracts?" Quayle asked.

"Now, how could I ask him that, dear boy?" Dunning protested. "I'm afraid you're unlucky. You can't watch everybody going in and out of public lavatories. You'd be picked up for soliciting and you-know-what." Dunning sniggered. "And how'd you know who'd picked up the papers without searching them all? Our man's damnably elusive, eh!" Dunning was enjoying himself. "You might as well catch the next London plane."

"I'll give it till tomorrow." Quayle hung up. Dunning was right. How did you catch somebody who recovered a package from a locked cubicle? Yet, Murphy alias Faulds couldn't leave those contracts too long in case something happened. As he ate the uninspired menu of shrimps, stewed mutton and bread-and-butter pudding, Quayle turned the question through every angle. One thing puzzled him: this Faulds was a curious IRA man to arrange a pick-up in central Belfast, where everybody risked being searched by police. By playing over the moves Faulds would have to make and analyzing each one, the glimmering of a plan came to him. That night he paid his bill and packed his valise.

He rose early, deposited his bag at the airline terminal and took post across from the Europa. At nine, Dunning emerged. Quayle followed fifty yards behind. Halfway to the public lavatories, the journalist slipped into a phone box and rang the attendant. "Now listen carefully," he said. "I'm a detective. In a minute, a man wearing a grey felt hat, checked sports jacket and brown trousers will come in and go straight to your number three toilet to hide a packet."

"Is this like some sort of a joke you're after playing, mister?" the attendant asked.

"No, everything will happen as I've said. Keep calm and watch the man, but don't attempt to stop him. He may be armed."

"What'll he be leaving in the toilet—a bomb?"

"No, it's not a bomb," Quayle assured him. "As soon as he leaves, put an out of order notice on that toilet and lock the door. Do nothing else. Is that clear?"

"Ay, mister, it's clear."

"I'll see you in five minutes."

Quayle arrived as Dunning was leaving. He entered and approached the bewildered attendant, a grey-faced man with a limp. "Open the door," he ordered and the man complied, then watched the journalist remove the cistern head and extract the dripping bundle.

"B'jeezus, you were right."

"We will have to put a tail on the man who's coming to collect this package," Quayle said curtly. He studied the glass-partitioned lodge where the attendant handed out soap and towels. "You'll have to take me on as your assistant for the day," he said and the man shrugged. Quayle donned a white coat and installed himself in the lodge to watch the constant traffic of men through the lavatory. Nobody gave the out of order notice on the toilet a second glance. At lunchtime, as he drank the beer and ate the sandwiches the old attendant fetched for them both, he began to wonder if Faulds had somehow got wind of his presence in Belfast and was lying low.

Just after three, a tall young man with abundant blond hair and matching beard, wearing dark glasses, entered the lavatory. At the out of order sign, he hesitated for a moment, then went into the urinal. Only when he had satisfied himself the place had emptied did he approach the attendants and point to the sign. "Not another bomb, I hope," he asked. He had a cultured Belfast accent.

"Thank the Lord God, no, sir," replied the attendant, briefed by Quayle. "It's an overflow and we've been after cutting the water." He lowered his voice. "We did like think it was a bomb. Some idiot jammed the cistern and we went for the bomb merchants."

"They couldn't fix it?"

"No, the ball valve's bust. They took away a package in case it was dangerous, like."

Quayle picked up a mop and pail, then slipped out of the lodge and the lavatory to position himself twenty yards from the gate. As Murphy alias Faulds showed at the top of the steps, the journalist got off half a dozen quick snaps with the miniature automatic camera he carried, aiming at the bearded face. Faulds spotted him and turned as if to challenge him, then shielded his face with his hands and ran off, sprinting through the crowd on Callendar Street. But Quayle had taken another couple of profile shots.

In the lodge, Quayle dressed and picked up the plastic bundle. Shaking the attendant's hand, he pressed a five-pound note into it. "Your bravery and cooperation were magnificent," he said grandly. "But not a word to anybody about what happened."

Within two hours, Quayle was sitting back at his Fleet Street desk. In another half-hour, he had a set of pictures before him; three of them would print well and showed Murphy-Faulds in full-face and profile. From the contracts, he found Murphy's full name and his relationship with Liam Faulds as well as the film-option terms. When he had written the story of how he trapped Faulds and captioned the pictures and contract, he dumped the lot on Jack Gibbon's desk.

Gibbon was staring hard at something like an architect's drawing-board draped with blank facsimile newspaper pages; he was scheming and drafting the page one layout for that Sunday. He grabbed the sheaf of papers and photos. "So, this is the IRA's Shamrock Pimpernel," he said, spreading the pictures and contract on the board; he scanned the story several times, clicking his dentures and sucking at a cigarette. Then, with an enormous black pencil, he boldly marked "Faulds Story" across two columns on the layout sheet with two pictures of Murphy-Faulds and a cross-reference to the inside page where they would run the contract pictures. He shot his journalist a sour glance. "We're playing it big not because it's not a bad tale, but because we've invested a fortune in your salary and expenses for these flimsy facts." His voice rasped even more. "Now, when are you going to knock the head off this literary boil? What I want's the story behind the story."

"Give me another week, and another couple of hundred," Quayle replied, and carried his expenses chit from the office. At no time did he think of his promise to Dunning to hold the story until it had been vetted, or reproach himself for stealing the contracts. Quayle would have argued, tongue-in-cheek, that his duty to his readers and democracy overrode his social scruples and private morality. Anyway, his hunch whispered the whole Liam Faulds story was crooked from beginning to end.

17

At eight o'clock on Sunday morning, when Anne Gilchrist came on duty, the two *Sunday Herald* advertising bills
in the hospital foyer halted her in her stride. Even from ten
yards, she recognized the two pictures of Martin under flar-
ing headlines: THIS IS LIAM FAULDS. WHAT IRA SAY
ABOUT MYSTERY BEST-SELLING AUTHOR. Although she
had expected something like this, those bills jolted her. She
bought the *Herald* and two rival papers to conceal her interest, took the lift to the surgical wards where she worked and
went to the women's toilet to read the story quietly. One
thing scared her: that Quayle would link Faulds with Martin.
However, the journalist seemed to have gone no further than
believing Michael Murphy to be Liam Faulds. Moreover, he
had not mentioned a London end of the Faulds story. Nor
made any hint about Baldwin. Only the pictures were dangerous, but she assured herself that even people who knew
Martin well would hardly connect him with the bearded, bespectacled figure in the photos.

In her office, while typing the morning reports, she re-
hearsed the plan she had formulated. She must act now, or

never. Thank God she had copied the last pages of *An Accident of Birth*. How long before Quayle landed on her doorstep and exposed all of them? He had declared he would make another series of sensational discoveries about Faulds and the IRA in the next issues of the *Herald*. She trembled at the thought. "Anne—is somebody walking over your grave?" Looking up, she saw the ward sister's Irish eyes on her, and shook her head. During her lunch hour, she went to the public call boxes in the Hammersmith tube station to make her calls.

Martin had left his Belfast hotel on Friday afternoon and it took her three more tries before she located him in a boarding-house near the docks that he had used twice. Yes, he had seen the *Herald*, had rid himself of his beard, glasses, the lot and decided to lie low. He would stay a week in Strabane where nobody knew him clean-shaven.

"No, Martin, now just listen," she said. "We haven't got time for that. You've got to get out now and come home."

"Why now?" he asked, then added, "But that's a crazy idea. Have you spoken to Graeme?"

"No, and I don't have to," she replied. "You don't know the whole picture. Now listen and do just what I say. You've got to get home without being seen. I'll explain when we meet. I can't talk here. Take the train south and fly from the other capital and get a cab home from the airport, but wait till it's dark. If I'm not there, don't answer the phone to anybody . . . anybody. And don't ring Mr. B. on any account. Do you understand all that?"

"Yes, I've got that—but I don't see why all the panic. They've got no real evidence."

"You'll understand why when you get here. Just promise me you'll do what I've told you."

When Gilchrist gave the promise, she put down the phone. Next, she rang Baldwin. He had not seen the paper, but assured her he would go out straight away, buy a copy and phone her at the hospital. Anne returned to her work place, had coffee and a sandwich in the nurses' canteen and had installed herself at her desk when Baldwin rang. She asked him to hang up, then went to the public booth on the ward and rang him at his home.

"I've read it all several times," he said. "It doesn't mean all that much."

"But if they recognize Martin and start hounding him . . ."

"He denies everything and threatens to sue. Anyhow, get hold of him and order him to lie low where he is." Baldwin thought for a moment. "I wonder if he knows what's in the paper."

"I'd think there's no doubt. The *Herald* has a wide sale in Northern Ireland and everybody must have seen that yellow poster they put out. I heard somebody in the hospital say they'd advertised it on TV last night."

"That means Fleet Street will start taking a real interest again," Baldwin mused. "Find him and tell him on no account to come home. If he's worried he can always head west or cross the line."

"I'll try his number now," Anne promised. She let a whole hour go before ringing Baldwin again. When she got through to him, she lied, saying she had tried all the hotels he had ever stayed in, but could not locate Martin. "I discovered he'd booked out of his hotel on Friday, just after the newspaperman took the snaps. But he's in none of the other places. He might be anywhere. I hope he hasn't panicked."

"Just cross your fingers he's stayed away from here where they'd nail him," he said. "His best place is across the border. If you manage to track him down, tell him that."

"Who's this man Quayle?" she asked.

"A little Fleet Street thug who has been pulling Dunning's ears for a couple of weeks."

"Do you think it's true, what he stated in the paper—he's going to tell the full story soon?"

"If they'd had anything like the truth they'd have printed it today," Baldwin suggested. "I know Quayle's editor. I'll have a drink with him and see how much they really have discovered."

"What do I do if he tackles me?"

"Say nothing—don't let him needle you," Baldwin said. "But your best bet is to avoid him altogether." He went silent for a few moments, then resumed talking. "It would be better if we left town for a couple of days in the middle of the week when Quayle is trying to put his next week's sensation together. Couldn't you go sick for a couple of days, farm out Moira and meet me at the hotel near Thame?"

Anne thought quickly. Charing Cross owed her a week of days and anyway, she was doing very little work; several of the surgeons who normally filled their wards with patients had gone on holiday. She could easily fix two days off next week. "I'll try," she said "What days do you suggest?"

"Say Tuesday and Wednesday."

"I'm sure they'll agree. If they don't, I'll ring by tomorrow midday. Unless you hear from me, I'll meet you at the hotel on Tuesday evening." Anne replaced the receiver and left the phone booth; she did not go to her office but walked to a small café in King Street, deserted at that hour. Over a cup of tea and three cigarettes, she pondered her course of action. By now, she knew Baldwin well enough almost to divine what he was thinking. Martin had no need to stay in Ireland, indeed he was safer this side of the water, and Baldwin did not want him there merely to cover their tracks from Quayle. No, he wanted the opportunity to make love to her, to persuade her to break finally with Gilchrist and set up house with him. His game had become so obvious that she had twitted him several times about it, accusing him of keeping her husband in Ulster to leave them free to have their fun.

"David and Bathsheba—that's you and me," she said. "And Martin is Uriah the Hittite, dispatched into the battle area so that the king can take his pleasure."

"Ah! but there's a big difference," he countered. "David made sure Bathsheba's hubby got his fatal comeuppance in

142

the battle zone. Me? I've heaped wealth on your husband and even shared my art and my name with him."

"David and Bathsheba had to pay for their treachery."

"I've paid."

"What does that make me?" she murmured, giving a grin to conceal her real feelings.

Baldwin, she guessed, would use those two days in Thame to talk her into packing a bag and leaving for a long holiday with him; they would then both write to Martin explaining their decision, but assuring him it did not change their professional relationship. So, whatever moves Anne had planned to counter this proposal would have to be made this week. In a sense, Baldwin's out-of-town expedition and his invitation to her fitted into her scheme. With luck, Martin might arrive tonight and she could put her idea to him and ask if he would play his part. If he did not cooperate, she always had the alternative of accepting Baldwin's offer.

When she spoke to them in the hospital, they raised no objection to her request for several days off that week.

18

On Monday, Baldwin decided he would escape to Thame a day earlier and wait there for Anne. Gibbon, he knew, would not stop until he had exposed Faulds. He had met Quayle and at least a hundred people betrayed by him, ending with Dunning, who was still reeling from the shock of reading that article. Baldwin didn't feel like tangling with Quayle or anybody else at this moment; his fragile nerves would never have withstood such a confrontation after that long and exhausting writing stint on *An Accident of Birth*, plus the incessant hide-and-seek game he had been playing with Anne to keep their meetings secret from everyone and their love secret from Gilchrist. In mid-afternoon, he was packing when his doorbell rang. He ignored it. A few minutes later his phone went, and thinking Anne might want a word, he picked it up. Immediately he recognized Quayle's adenoidal voice. "I rang your doorbell, but you couldn't have heard."

"I heard," Baldwin snapped. "I'm busy and I'm not seeing anybody."

"It's only for a couple of minutes," Quayle murmured.

"Jack Gibbon thought I'd better see you about the Faulds business."

That statement set Baldwin thinking. Did they have something more to print? Something concerning himself? "Literally for a couple of minutes," he said. When Quayle arrived, he directed him into the living room and offered him a whisky, though pointedly refraining himself. "So, what does my friend Jack Gibbon want you to see me about?"

"Just what you know about the Faulds story." Quayle rinsed the whisky round his glass, swallowed some. "You've seen my last piece."

"I glanced at it," Baldwin admitted. "But you haven't proved this man Murphy you grabbed in Belfast has anything to do with Faulds."

"He's Faulds all right."

"Then you do have proof."

"We had a tip-off, which is why I went to Belfast."

"Ah! Who from?" Baldwin tried to keep his voice calm.

"An anonymous letter," Quayle said. "But from somebody who knew Faulds."

Baldwin lit a cigarette, trying to keep his hand steady. "I'd say you were way ahead of me and everybody else in that case."

"But Jack thought you might have run into somebody like Faulds in your Northern Ireland travels," Quayle said, unabashed. "One or two of your stories reminded us of *A Common Grave.*"

This man was trying to wrong-foot him. What had that anonymous note said? Who had written it? This snake *would* go to the cuttings and dig out his Ulster material. Yet, off the top of his head, he remembered nothing there to suggest it had inspired the novel. Quayle's reptilian eyes were fixed on his face, trying to unnerve him. So well he knew this type, weaseling in and out of personal tragedies, wrecking lives and careers with his half-truths and glib lies. "My stories were nothing like the novel, the way I read it," he muttered.

He rose to refill the journalist's glass, but this time helped himself to a large whisky. "Tell Jack I've never heard of Faulds or this man Murphy."

"Murphy's not his real name."

"But you said Murphy was Faulds."

"Faulds, Murphy—they're only names on a book or contract and mean nothing." Quayle was noting the way Baldwin gulped his whisky and chain-smoked cigarettes, snuffing them out after a couple of puffs. Gibbon had mentioned the writer was going through a sticky patch and they were pulping his books. Played out and jumpy as a trampoline man, he thought. Reaching into his wallet, he pulled out the Faulds pictures, displaying them on the coffee table. "Ever seen him before?" he asked.

"Hundreds of times," Baldwin replied, glancing at the shots. Seeing the other man's brows furrow with surprise, he grinned. "I've seen men like that all over Ireland. There are thousands of spud-faced Irishmen like him."

Undeterred, Quayle produced another set of pictures. "Try him without the beard and glasses," he proposed. A Fleet Street artist had removed the beard, moustache and glasses from the full-face and profile pictures. He looked like Gilchrist's passport picture, and had the *Herald* published these, some reader might have recognized the Ulsterman. Baldwin felt relieved he had warned Anne to keep her husband in Ireland, as far from Belfast as possible; but even so, he realized someone in Britain might pierce that beard-and-glasses disguise.

"I prefer him with the beard," he said, smiling. "But joking apart, I've never seen him, with or without beard."

"What did you think of the book?" Quayle asked, switching his tack.

"A great piece of writing, straight from the heart," Baldwin said. "It must have been difficult telling it like an eyewitness story, unless he was involved himself."

"What would you say—a professional writer or a gifted amateur?"

146

"There, you toss a coin."

"Everybody reckons it'll win the Eddystone Prize," Quayle said. "You're on the jury. Are you going to vote for it?"

"Ask me how long's a piece of string," Baldwin declared, standing up to signal the end of their discussion. He peered at his watch. "Sorry Quayle, but I've an out-of-town appointment and can't go on talking about literature. I wish you luck with this will-o'-the-wisp man, Faulds. Know something? I shall envy you if you run him to earth. I'd very much like to meet him myself." Ushering the little journalist to the door, he returned to finish packing. He cursed Jack Gibbon. That slimy homunculus of his gave him the creeps with his fork-tongued questions. Even conversing with him felt like looking a hooded cobra in the eye. Was he just bluffing about that anonymous note? Had Martin Gilchrist slipped up? Or revealed something he shouldn't to someone? Or was somebody else writing the script of this conspiracy as well as himself?

Within a quarter of an hour, Baldwin was driving through the London suburbs on the westbound motorway. As he cleared the strip building and headed into open country, his heart and mind seemed to shed a great burden. For ten months, he had lived a dual or triple existence that appeared to have fragmented his personality. Often, as he sat at his study desk, he wondered who he really was. Graeme Baldwin, Liam Faulds, even Martin Gilchrist? Or bits of all three. And during that verbal joust with Quayle, he sensed the little reporter was catching a whiff of something strange or suspicious in the air of his flat. Or something abnormal in his behavior. However, at this moment Baldwin felt it did not matter what the little reptile discovered. Let him dig and go on digging until he unearthed everything, exposed everything and everyone. For his part, Baldwin had grown tired of living out this masque he had scripted for himself and two other people to act before a credulous public of several millions. It had become a farce that had run long enough. This trick to redeem himself at the expense of people like poor Dunning had turned acid in his mouth. Some lies you could invent and tell and feel guilty about, then forget or stuff in an odd mental recess and repress. But he had been living his lie every minute of the day; and he had compounded his guilt by seducing Anne Gilchrist and cuckholding her husband, his other collaborator. Did he really love Anne, as he declared? Or had he merely been trying to assuage some of the guilt he experienced by asking her to run away with him and become his wife? These questions he could not answer. Nor would he ever answer them until he had sloughed off the skins of Liam Faulds and his other doppelgänger, Gilchrist.

A few miles before Oxford, he left the motorway and drove to the small hotel on the edge of Thame; it looked across an infinity of flat country, which gave him that cherished sense of isolation. Anne apart, not a soul knew he was there. He had a quiet dinner and watched a TV film in his room.

Next day, he drove into Oxford to wander round the colleges and browse in second-hand bookshops, where he acquired half a dozen old prints. Even there, Liam Faulds pursued him, his eye lighting on paperback displays of *A Common Grave* in High Street bookstores. Returning to the hotel after lunch, he found a message from Anne. She would ring again at six. He fretted until the phone went. She apologized profusely but she could not join him that night. Moira was running a temperature and had been ordered to bed. It was nothing serious and would probably clear up by next day. She would catch a morning or early afternoon train. No, she had heard nothing from Mr. Q. No news, either, from abroad.

Baldwin filled in the evening working on his diary. From the outset of the Faulds masquerade, he had noted every event concerning himself and the Gilchrists. When it came time to reveal the hoax, he would construct a factual novel called *The Life and Death of Liam Faulds*. Several long chapters, already written, were sitting with the rest of the

Faulds material in his Kensington bank vault. That book would cause a sensation. Just to watch its effect on the faces of Dunning and Seaborne would compensate him for all the pain and effort. Quayle, too, would have a red face, exposing Faulds in the person of Murphy. In six weeks, when the Eddystone Prize jury voted for *A Common Grave*, he would vote against, just for the record. Being unable to produce Faulds, Dunning would have to reject the award. Then Faulds would issue a statement saying he would have refused the prize, being opposed to literary charades mostly rigged by publishers and their parasitic authors. That would sell a million more copies of *A Common Grave* and ensure the success of *An Accident of Birth*.

Next morning, Anne rang. She would arrive at midday, but could not stay the night. Baldwin met her at Oxford and drove back to have lunch in their room. A neighbour was looking after Moira for several hours. However, Anne had bad news, which had brought her down to consult him. Martin was returning tomorrow; he considered he ran less risk of being recognized in London and had decided to lie low in Fulham until the *Sunday Herald* called off its hunt for Faulds.

"He's a bloody fool," Baldwin exclaimed, though more out of exasperation at having his pleasure spoiled than at Gilchrist's panic-stricken move. "But he may be right in thinking he's safer at home," he conceded. "Nobody's going to connect him with those pictures taken in Belfast, and we can keep an eye on him here."

"But, Graeme darling, it means I've got to get back before he arrives," she said.

"That's all right. I'll book out and run you back to London."

She would not hear of this suggestion. "That's not the way to do it," she said. "I don't know how or why, but I think he suspects something between us. He sounded grim when he spoke to me and I got the impression he'd either heard or guessed about us."

"Well, why not seize the chance to have it out with him once and for all—clear the air?"

"I've wondered about that, but I don't think it's wise," she replied. "You don't know Martin. He's quite capable of doing something idiotic—even running to the *Sunday Herald* and blabbing about everything. You must give me a couple of days to explain things, gently, to him and make him understand. I can handle him better on my own, especially if you're not around for him to pick a fight with."

He argued he could hold his own with Gilchrist, but she stifled his objections, persuading him as she always could, no matter how weak her reasoning, by enticing him into bed with her and making love. Whatever doubts he might have had about her love for him, she dispelled that afternoon. "Why argue when we may not see each other alone for weeks and weeks, darling?" she whispered as she allowed him to undress her and let her tawny hair fall over her shoulders. For a long time they lay with their nude bodies pressed against each other in that room with the grey twilight filtering through the closed curtains. Then Anne began to explore his face and the whole of his body as though trying to impress every one of their contours, their bones, their skin, their secret recesses on her mind by way of her fingertips; or as though trying to release some concealed catch that would throw open a labyrinth of new and more powerful sensations for them. Each touch, each caress of those curiously blunt fingers sent a frisson through Baldwin; she ran her lips over his face and his lips, darting her tongue between them. Always before, her passion began to spill over when they started this love-play; but now she was checking herself, waiting for the right moment, the precise touch that would trigger their mutual passion. When it came, she astounded Baldwin with the rage and violence of her desire for him. Even he felt caught up in this physical and sensual storm in which they yielded everything of themselves, carried by their excitement into another dimension, beyond time and the confines of their small room. And when he lay, slack and void of energy, she encouraged him again, and again, until he could no longer conceive of matching her sexual appetite. With another woman, he might have felt inferior; but it flattered him that Anne wanted him so much and seemed to store up her desire for weeks during the periods they could not see each other.

Baldwin dropped into a deep sleep. At five-thirty, she shook him awake, whispering that she must catch a train just after six from Oxford. Dressing quickly, he poured them both a stiff whisky from his bottle, then drove into Oxford. When he stopped the car in front of the station, she kissed him on the lips, then looked at him straight. "Graeme darling, promise me you'll give me until Saturday to discuss things with Martin and make our peace with him. It's important for both of us, but it's very important for me. Promise?"

"Of course, I promise," he said, and she kissed him again. He sat watching her skip through the booking-hall until she disappeared towards the London platform.

19

That night and part of the following day, Baldwin worked over his notes for the book on the Faulds conspiracy. In the afternoon, he trudged across country but drenching rain drove him back to the hotel, increasing his longing for London and his study. An urban writer, he had grown up in a landscape of slum dwellings, tawdry shops and mean streets with a view of London bridges and the miasmic Thames stench in his nostrils. Nature hardly bothered him; it figured little in his novels and he maintained that, like Picasso, had they shoved him into solitary for life, his writing would not have changed. He dredged his inspiration from studying men and women amid their artifacts rather than from the land, sea and sky and flora and fauna; he preferred the clean geometry of a jet contrail to cloud patterns. To him, those bulging cumuli rolling over Oxfordshire looked like so much phlegm and the rain so much spit. However, he would stick to his promise and suffer until Saturday.

After dinner, he felt tired and went to bed early. At eight o'clock the next morning a maid brought breakfast, which he ate in bed before leafing through *The Times* he had ordered. Suddenly, a known face stared out at him. Anthony Lewis. Under a headline that set his mind spinning: BARRISTER FOUND DEAD IN BLAZING HOME. Baldwin skimmed the story feverishly. It said the fire had started through a faulty heater or a short-circuit. Lewis had tried to summon help before suffocating in the smoke-filled house. Baldwin did not bother to read about the barrister's famous cases and career. He phoned for his bill and started to dress. As he ran a razor over his beard he suddenly felt light-headed, and disconnected even from that wan face in his mirror.

Lewis had that document in his safe. If somebody opened it and read the contract he had written in his own hand, notarized and signed by Lewis, the Liam Faulds game would end with a bang before he could stop it. Was fate trying to kick his teeth in? First Quayle, and now this. Lewis said he'd put the paper in his safe at home. So Baldwin must get there before anybody else and retrieve that agreement. He rang Lewis's chambers, where his clerk supplied the name of the barrister's solicitor, a certain Norman S. Kerwin of a City of London firm. Before leaving Thame, Baldwin called Kerwin, who tut-tutted about the impropriety and illegality of searching Lewis's safe, now under state control like all his other possessions. Baldwin insisted that the letter bore his name and was his property, and finally the solicitor agreed to meet him at Lewis's house around midday.

Baldwin drove to the barrister's Bayswater house, blackened and blistered; two first-floor windows gaped open, like the front door. On the pavement outside, a local newspaperman recognized the novelist, who explained Lewis had been his lawyer and a personal friend. Over a drink in the nearest pub, the pressman recounted what he had picked up from detectives.

Lewis's housekeeper, who lived in the basement, had raised the alarm at three o'clock Thursday morning. Since the front door was locked and bolted from the inside, firemen broke through it and the two bedroom windows. Lewis was found dead in his bedroom with a head injury. He was

153

thought to have woken when smoke seeped upstairs. By then, the fire had melted all the fuses and he had no light. According to the detectives, he was trying to open or break the window when smoke overcame him and he fell and hit his head on a night table.

"Where did the fire start?"

"They think in the downstairs library," the reporter said. "He had a convector heater there, and they think a curtain or a piece of paper fell on the grill and the element overheated. Seems the fire spread to the bathroom, the kitchen, then upstairs."

"No sign of arson?"

"They think it's an open-and-shut case," the reporter said.

Baldwin thanked him. Wandering along Craven Street, he found a café and had a coffee and a sandwich to settle his nerves more than anything while he waited for the solicitor. Something nagged at his mind. How did a meticulous man like Tony Lewis come to foul a convector fire with a curtain or papers? Why a fire on a fine summer evening, except for the rain? Why didn't he spot the fire before his housekeeper, two floors below him?

Kerwin wore bottle-lens spectacles and, in Baldwin's view, had a horn-rimmed mind to match. "Highly irregular, all this," he sniffed. "Why the urgency over this paper?"

"It happens to be a very private document that I entrusted to my lawyer and he has put it in a sealed envelope with my name on it."

Kerwin insisted on seeking police permission and speaking to the Inland Revenue before acting. He let them into the house, stinking of charred furniture and scorched plaster. Little damage had occurred in the living room and the safe opened easily; it contained several hundred pounds in notes, some personal papers, insurance policies, a copy of Lewis's will and several diaries. But no envelope.

"Yet he assured me he'd keep it in his safe, here," Baldwin got out.

Another search yielded nothing. Lewis had obviously hidden the paper elsewhere. Why hadn't he made a note, or warned him? Kerwin promised to contact him when the paper came to light.

Before leaving, Baldwin slipped into the library to examine the burnt-out electric fire; a French window opened on to a sunken garden and he tried the handle. Locked like the other door. Everything pointing to an accident. But where was that paper?

Once home he went straight to his desk, deciding to lose himself by writing several pages of his novel within a novel about the Faulds case, the more so since that missing contract or the rat-faced Quayle might reveal at any minute Liam Faulds was none other than Graeme Baldwin, the bestselling author. A pity. Out of the Faulds plot, he had fashioned two books and three-quarters of a third; he could easily have kept the name and the game going for years, doing a Faulds and a Baldwin alternately.

When he had typed several pages, he unlocked the cupboard behind him to place them beside the manuscript and exercise books of *An Accident of Birth*. Going automatically to close the door, his hand halted as though paralyzed; his shocked mind perceived the cupboard lay empty apart from his automatic pistol, ammunition and the tape machine on which he had recorded Anne's story and source material for the second Faulds book.

Everything had gone. His typescript of *An Accident of Birth*, the pile of exercise books into which Anne had copied the book, the dozen or so cassettes containing her narrative and his questions. What had she done with them? Had she suddenly grown scared somebody—Quayle maybe—would discover them and arranged another hiding place? Baldwin opened the desk drawer where he kept his diaries of the Faulds case. They, too, had disappeared! But surely Anne would have phoned to warn him if their secret had been threatened. What was she playing at? He must find out. Seizing the phone, he dialled her home number, but she did not answer. At the hospital, the girl on Surgical Reception informed him that Mrs. Gilchrist had gone sick on Tuesday but would probably return to duty on the following Monday. Sick! But he had seen her on Wednesday and she had mentioned nothing about that, either. Baldwin threw the handset back into its cradle. His head throbbed and he felt that peculiar aura preceding one of his migraines. However, he dismissed the idea of masking it with aspirin. He must think straight. Anthony Lewis was dead, and with him had perished the secret whereabouts of that document. Baldwin's mind retreated to that sunlit afternoon just under a year ago with himself and Lewis under the Indian bean tree in Temple Gardens; Lewis's gravelly whisper echoed in his head. "Have you weighed up the possibility that Gilchrist might blackmail you if the book goes well?" His mind recalled, too, how Anne had interrogated him, oh! so gently, about the third contract and the rest of the papers. Why, she had even suggested Lewis might betray them all!

But how could they, either Anne or Gilchrist, blackmail or betray him? He had built in so many precautions. There was all that material he had placed in his strongbox at the bank. That would give them away. A panic notion hit him and he pulled his key-ring from his pocket. No, the strongbox key with its twisted, fluted combination was still there. Anyway, the bank official in charge of those boxes knew him and had to use his own passkey before Baldwin used his to open that box. Father Regan? No, he knew Baldwin only as an intermediary for Gilchrist and could not therefore testify that Baldwin was the real author of the Faulds texts. However, there was that drunken solicitor, Ryan in Dublin. He knew enough of the story to blab. Or did he? Reflecting hard, Baldwin remembered an embarrassed Gilchrist confessing he had used only the name Murphy on that phoney Dublin agreement with the nonexistent Faulds. So, Ryan could prove nothing; he would accept Murphy as the main conspirator, he would always back an Irishman against an Englishman and would not twitch a muscle if Murphy stabbed a novelist called Baldwin in the back. In any case, he would not talk since he had perjured himself and would be struck off for producing false affidavits declaring he had met Murphy and Faulds. But no, Baldwin told himself. It was unthinkable. Anne couldn't, she wouldn't ever try to betray him. Not after those hours in that Thame bedroom two days ago.

Yet, as he sat there, his head thumping with the effort of unravelling the puzzle he himself had constructed, his doubts began to crystallize. Of course they could claim authorship, swearing that he had merely corrected the typescript and helped them edit it. Gilchrist had used the name Murphy because he could now declare he wanted to protect himself, the real author. A clever move that one, so early in the game. Why had Anne insisted that he return on Saturday? Obviously because the banks were shut on that day. He glanced at his watch. Four-thirty. They were already closed. Nevertheless, he rang and spoke to the clerk in charge of the strongboxes, saying he must meet him urgently. Within a quarter of an hour, he had marched down Camden Hill and was following the bank official through two iron grilles to his own box. When the man turned his key and stepped, discreetly, out of sight, Baldwin used his own key and opened the box.

That, too, lay empty.

Baldwin beckoned the official. "But how can this be empty?" he exclaimed, pointing to the box. "Last time I saw it, that box was crammed full of papers. Who emptied it?"

"But Mr. Baldwin, you yourself sent someone to collect everything in the box."

"I certainly didn't," Baldwin said. "Who came, and when?"

"It was a young lady, sir. I remember her distinctly. She came on Tuesday afternoon with a letter signed by you. She said she was your secretary."

"And you took her word for it!"

"Not at all, sir," the official said. "We checked your signature against our records and it matched. Then we phoned your home to confirm your instructions. The young lady even suggested this and I phoned myself and spoke to you."

"You mean somebody imitating my voice," Baldwin snapped. He was recalling how Gilchrist had once revealed that both he and his wife had done amateur theatricals in Belfast, and that evening he had shown off his skills as a mimic.

"But it couldn't have been," the bank official stammered. "It was your phone number and the man sounded exactly like you. You said you were ill and to give the young lady what was in the box." He pulled out a packet, took a cigarette, lit it and drew several gulps of smoke. "What were we to do? We had your signature, the young lady had the strongbox key and the man who answered the phone had a voice like yours and knew what was in the letter she carried."

"What was she like, this woman?"

When he had reflected for a moment, the man said, "She was tall with very dark hair and she wore those large, tortoise-shell glasses. She was pretty."

"Did she have an Irish accent?"

"No, I remember her voice."

"You must have obtained a signature for your book before you opened the box," Baldwin said. They went back upstairs and he studied the signature in the book under Tuesday's date. It had something of Anne's ornate handwriting, that signature. But the woman had signed herself Patricia Howard.

Baldwin walked out of the bank in a complete spin, hardly knowing where he was going, let alone what action to take. Anne Gilchrist had used her dramatic talents to disguise herself and her voice and fool the bank clerk. But he could only blame himself; he should have read the signs when she quizzed him that first night in her flat and added her little personal touches to his plan. She had duped him all along the line. It was she who had set Quayle on the track with her anonymous note, knowing it would lead to the exposure of Faulds. When that happened, they would claim authorship and make themselves a fortune. Now, he could not produce the vital bits of evidence to prove he had written the Liam Faulds books. It seemed the Gilchrists had him cornered. She had figured everything out, perhaps in the weeks just after the plot began, when Gilchrist disobeyed instructions and gave Ryan, the solicitor, his false name. She had been working against him all the time while he, the idiot, thought she had fallen for him. When he believed he was making the running, she was, in fact, leading him on. She had even lured him, so cunningly, to write that second novel, aware it would buttress their claim to have written both the Faulds books. Who would dispute they had a fitting background to write *A Common Grave?* And the second novel, *An Accident of Birth*, was part of their own story. Now, he understood why she had been prodding him over these last weeks to complete the book, and why she had rushed to copy the final pages.

He reckoned himself no mean hand at devising plots and thought he had written the perfect Liam Faulds scenario. But Anne Gilchrist had outplotted him.

20

On the pavement a few yards from the bank, Baldwin halted so abruptly that two people collided with him and cursed. A thought had hit the novelist: one man would know the truth as soon as he had made things plain—Keith Dunning. He almost ran to the tube station in Kensington High Street and phoned Gresham and Holt. No, a secretary answered, Mr. Dunning had already left and would probably be spending the weekend at his country house near Gerrards Cross. A cab took Baldwin to his car and he drove through Hammersmith to the westbound motorway. At that hour, even on the motorway, he could not do the journey in less than three-quarters of an hour. Dunning lived in some style; his Georgian house sat on two acres of ground on which he had built a swimming pool, tennis courts and even a small point-to-point course for the children and their ponies. Baldwin had to make small-talk with Dunning's dull, county wife, then wrestle clear of their two slobbering boxer dogs before he got the editor on his own. "I've something to tell you, Keith," he said. "In private."

Dunning shot him a curious glance, then led them to his

writing den, a library full of the books he had edited and some rare first editions. "Nice to see you, ol' chum," he murmured. "To what do we owe the honour?"

Baldwin lit a cigarette with a shaky hand. "Keith, I have a confession to make . . . a confession you won't like at all . . . won't like at all." He paused, then blurted out, "I am Liam Faulds."

Dunning's head came up, his face dropped a notch for a moment, then his shoulders quivered, his head went back and, for the first time in his life, Baldwin saw him laughing, then guffawing. "I'm frightfully sorry, ol' boy, but the way you said it, I thought for a brief minute you meant it."

"But I do mean it, you bloody fool, I do mean it," Baldwin roared and Dunning held up both hands, palms outward, to calm the novelist. Without saying anything, the editor went outside and returned with a bottle of Scotch and two glasses. He poured the liquor generously into the glasses, handing one to Baldwin. "Have a snifter of that, Graeme, and you'll feel better."

"I don't need that, and there's nothing wrong with me and I feel fine," Baldwin replied, though he accepted the Scotch and gulped it down, neat. "What I've just told you is true. I am Liam Faulds. I thought the whole thing up and enlisted the Gilchrists to help me fool everybody."

"The Gilchrists? Who're they?"

"He's a freelance journalist and his wife's a hospital secretary. They're both Irish. Gilchrist's the man you met in Ulster umpteen times, the man who appeared in the *Sunday Herald* pictures."

"But that man's name is Murphy," Dunning objected.

"An alias, like Liam Faulds," Baldwin came back. "And Liam Faulds does not exist outside my mind." He held out his glass and Dunning poured him another whisky, his face now pensive. "I can tell you where and when you met Gilchrist alias Murphy around Belfast or on the Northern Ireland border and how he sent you on the fool's errand to Rathlin Island—all that."

161

"Yes, Graeme, but don't you remember, I told you all that stuff myself?" Dunning shook his head, incredulously, at Baldwin's memory lapse. "You came to the office the first time and I told you about Murphy, then I brought you up to date on the other trips. In fact, you seemed as interested as we were in Liam Faulds."

"Of course I was since I invented him," Baldwin said curtly. "I was checking up to keep Gilchrist informed of your reactions and your moves when he was in Ireland." From Dunning's signals, Baldwin became aware he was still talking too loudly. "I planned the whole thing, I tell you—down to the last detail." He helped himself to another Scotch, swallowing it at a gulp. "I'm only confessing now because the Gilchrists have stabbed me in the back."

"How could they do that?" As he asked the question, Dunning was studying the novelist's flushed face and nervous movements. A funny character, Baldwin. Always envying other writers their success and their sales, always rubbing up rival novelists the wrong way, always getting on the bad side of his colleagues on the Eddystone Prize jury.

"How!" Baldwin repeated. "They've stolen all my original typescripts and the notes in my own hand."

"But the manuscript of *A Common Grave* was handwritten, not typewritten," Dunning came back.

"That was to fool you—which it did," Baldwin said, irritably. "Gilchrist's wife did the copying."

"So the papers have all disappeared and you have no proof," Dunning murmured with a trace of indulgence in his voice.

"No, I do have proof," Baldwin exclaimed. He approached the other man and lowered his voice. "This is very much between you and me." He paused, then said, "I have written a second Liam Faulds book."

"Oh! That's interesting," Dunning drawled. "What have you called that?"

"It's called *An Accident of Birth*," Baldwin said, now sure he had Dunning's sympathy. "It's the story of the Gilchrists and their mongol child, Michael, though we've changed the names."

"I know," Dunning said.

"You know!" Baldwin shouted. "How can you know?"

Without a word, Dunning disappeared through the door. A few minutes later, he returned with a carton which he dumped on his desk. Raising the flap, he revealed the whole pile of exercise books that had vanished from Baldwin's flat. "They're exactly the same as the last—in the same handwriting," Dunning commented, picking one up.

Baldwin grabbed the school jotter out of the publisher's hand and flipped through its pages, which he had watched Anne copy over the months. He threw the book back into the carton, then seized Dunning by the jacket lapels. "Where did you get them?" he shouted.

Dunning detached himself from Baldwin's grasp and stepped back a few paces. "*Mystère, mystère*," he murmured. "They were deposited on our reception desk yesterday by some unknown person while the secretary's back was turned."

Baldwin pointed to the exercise books. "I wrote that story, every line of it—and the slut pinched it."

"The slut is who?"

"Gilchrist's wife," Baldwin whispered. He shook his head in disbelief and bewilderment. "I thought I was in love with her, the bitch, and this is what she did." He turned his gaze on Dunning, who was watching him intently. "I can tell you the whole story of *An Accident of Birth*, if you like." Then, chapter by chapter, he outlined the book while Dunning listened with marked attention and without once uttering. However, when Baldwin had finished, he put one question: "Are you sure you haven't been suborning one of the two girls in our office who have been copying all these texts?"

"What do you take me for?" Baldwin cried. "You've known me for more than fifteen years and I've never lifted a line from another writer in my life."

163

"I might believe you, Graeme," Dunning said. "But if you've no written proof, then these people, whoever they are, can claim you merely helped them edit their manuscript."

"And bloody idiots like you will obviously believe them," Baldwin said. "I'm telling the truth, I tell you." Without any warning, he swept the cardboard box off the desk and was making for the door with it when Dunning barred his path. "Put that down, Graeme," he said, quietly. As Baldwin hesitated, he took the box out of his arms. "Look, he said, "let's talk about all this when we've simmered down and can thrash everything out quietly and calmly. Say, in my office on Monday, eh? I'm sure we can sort everything out then." Putting his arm through Baldwin's, he walked with him to the car in front of the house. "Sure you can steer a straight line, Graeme?" he asked with a grin. Baldwin looked at him, nodding dumbly. He got in, slammed the car into gear and kicked up a shower of gravel as he accelerated away from the house.

Dunning watched him disappear, then went indoors, shaking his head sadly. Baldwin had every symptom of a man who was cracking up and might do something stupid. He hoped the novelist would not repeat that act of folly or desperation a few years ago just after his divorce. Then, he had eaten a fistful of pills and swallowed a bottle of gin and they'd had to put him on kidney dialysis for two days. How many authors had he witnessed turning funny like that, claiming to have written somebody else's best-seller and backing their claims with what sounded like truth! Some of them would even affirm on oath they had written the Bible, Shakespeare and Homer. Why did he, Dunning, have to pick them—these cloak-and-dagger merchants like Faulds-Murphy and temperamental types like Baldwin, who looked halfway round the bend these days? He prayed Baldwin would lift himself out of his paranoia before the Eddystone Prize lunch. It would make things difficult for *A Common*

Grave and everybody connected with it if Baldwin suddenly stood up before the jury and announced he had written it.

Dunning sat down and poured himself another whisky, which he scrutinized a long time, thinking he was growing too fond of the stuff since the Faulds affair began. He sipped the liquor slowly as he opened the first exercise book of *An Accident of Birth*, which he had brought home to read that weekend at his leisure. An hour later, his wife had to call him half a dozen times for dinner before he surfaced into the present, so deeply had he plunged into the book and identified with its characters. Without a shadow of doubt it was another winner.

21

Baldwin felt emotionally drained, almost too tired to keep his eyes and mind on the road. That day had already lasted an eternity, from the moment he saw the headlines about Lewis. Just beyond Denham, he stopped at a wayside restaurant to eat a snack and drink a glass of beer, which revived him a little. When he reflected, he had to hand it to Anne Gilchrist; she had given his foolproof plot a new and original twist by planning to blow up his own booby trap in his face. Somehow, he had to foil her plot. As he drove the rest of the way in darkness, the act of staring into his headlight beam seemed to focus his mind on the problem. What prevented him from recovering that initial contract through Lewis's solicitor? It had his and the Gilchrists' signatures as well as the barrister's verification of them. With that and the reconstruction of every move in his scheme, he could still prove authorship of the Liam Faulds books. However, he must act quickly without bothering about that ninny, Dunning. On Monday, he would initiate legal steps to halt publication of *A Common Grave* under the pseudonym Liam Faulds; he would also cancel Gilchrist's share of the revenue from royalties and rights. Once home, he must check to see if he still possessed the original copy of the third-person novel on which he had based *A Common Grave*. That would prove its genealogy. Another inspiration hit him: if everything else failed, he could always recruit Quayle and confess everything to him in Jack Gibbon's presence. They would dig and ferret and eventually break down the Gilchrists. No, the game was nothing like lost.

Parking the car, he marched briskly to his flat; he let himself in and switched on the hall light. Even before he got to the living room, he caught a whiff of that cloying perfume and wondered why he had never noticed how cheap and vulgar it was—and the whore who used it. As he reached the study door, he glimpsed her standing by the window, in her coat, alone. However, when he took a step towards her, the front door clicked behind him and he turned to discover Gilchrist entering the living room from the hall. "We thought you might make a bolt for it when you saw me," Anne Gilchrist murmured.

"It's what I should have done nearly a year ago," he retorted. Fixing his gaze on Gilchrist, who had entered the study, he said, "When did you find out your wife was a whore?"

In reply, Gilchrist clenched his gloved right fist and drew back as though to strike Baldwin, but his wife snapped, "No, Martin, no violence, nothing anybody would see."

"She's also a bitch, your wife," Baldwin said. "I should have known better than take the word of a woman who betrayed the trust of her own innocent child, then sold herself." He pointed at Gilchrist. "And you're no better. You're a couple of thieves and traitors."

"And you don't think you're a thief as well?" Anne Gilchrist countered, her voice full of venom. "You thieved part of our lives and you thieved a part of me, and you forced me to betray Martin, who trusted you—all for your own ego." Why had Baldwin never before perceived the brutal clench of her face and those eyes, hard as date stones? She was still talking, sneering at him. "You don't know what it felt like just to have you touch me and paw me all over."

"I'll give you this, you're a good actress. You fooled me, and you fooled the bank clerk, and you'll fool him, too." Baldwin thumbed at Gilchrist, then said to him, "She'll use you for her little plot, then toss you aside the minute it suits her."

"I love Martin," she said.

"But not half as much as you love his money, and mine," Baldwin said.

"That money's as much ours as yours," she said. "We're only taking back what rightfully belongs to us."

"Nothing belongs to you," Baldwin said. "You'll find that out on Monday." Without thinking, he outlined what he intended to do: stop publication of all Faulds books; annul their joint bank account and have the book contracts rewritten by the publisher; yet, he would concede them their twenty percent agent's fee on *A Common Grave* since he had contracted to do this, even though they had just broken their agreement; he would publish letters in the press and, later on, his own account of the Faulds affair.

Anne Gilchrist heard him out, then smiled and shook her head. "You can't do any of those things," she said. "Because you cannot prove you wrote those books. Everything of yours has been burned and the only thing that remains of those books is in my handwriting."

"I've just come from seeing Dunning. He believes me and he'll back my testimony against yours."

"Dunning's a fool who believes anything," she snapped. "You said so yourself, and he's proved it over the past year. If he admitted now you were Liam Faulds, he'd be admitting his own stupidity and gullibility."

Baldwin had to admire her logic and her character reading as well as her intelligence. "Haven't you forgotten one thing—the paper Anthony Lewis had in his safe? When his solicitors eventually find the contract and read it, the game will be up for both of you."

"Nobody will find that paper," Gilchrist said, speaking for the first time.

"Martin . . ." she cautioned.

Gilchrist shrugged, then said, "We might as well tell him." He grinned at Baldwin. "Nobody will ever see that paper, for the simple reason it doesn't exist any more."

Baldwin gazed at him, his mind wrestling with that last statement, fitting it into the series of sinister hints he had gathered at Lewis's house that morning. "So it was you two who killed Tony Lewis," he gasped. Suddenly his legs felt weak, watery; he placed his hands on the desk to steady himself, then moved around it to sit in his chair. Dinning through his head was the disclosure of that callous murder for which he, Baldwin, must accept some of the blame. Had he not contrived most of this plot and involved the barrister in it? Now the fact that Gilchrist had admitted the murder, almost boasted about it, could mean one thing: they meant to murder him, too. "So Lewis let you into his flat Wednesday evening and you hit him on the head, rifled his safe, then put a match to the house. Was that it?"

"Mr. Lewis died in a fire," Anne Gilchrist said quietly. "That's what the police say, so who are we to disagree. Before he died, he did meet us and gave us the envelope with his copy of the contract in it."

Baldwin looked at them. His eyes went to the telephone, but she had guessed what was going through his mind. "It's unplugged," she said.

"You've quite a talent for crime," Baldwin muttered. "I suppose I'm the other man on your murder list and you've figured out how to get rid of me and make it look like suicide."

"You've tried it once—unsuccessfully," she said. "Why shouldn't you succeed this time?"

"The coroner mightn't agree with you."

"He will when he sees the note you have typed on your own machine, and the police find only your fingerprints on the notepaper."

"Oh! yes, the bit of headed paper you asked me to pass you a week ago. And the signature?"

"We fooled the bank clerk, so why not the police?"

"I'm the real fool," Baldwin said, bitterly. "I thought you came to Thame to see me. What did you come to do—put back the strongbox key on my ring in case I missed it and suspected you'd pinched it? And, of course, you needed to keep me out of play for another day so that you could kill Lewis." Neither of the Gilchrists replied. Baldwin looked at Anne. "You've fooled everybody so far, but there's one man you won't fool."

"Who's that?" she said. As she spoke, her eyes flickered towards Gilchrist, who had moved round behind Baldwin and now pulled something out of the bookshelves on the other side of the novelist.

"Quayle," Baldwin said. "Quayle will never stop until he has the real story. He'll get at the truth."

Those were his last words. He heard a whipcrack sound, then his head filled to bursting with an enormous detonation that seemed to hoist him, physically, out of his chair, dash him against the wall, then hurl him into the cold darkness outside.

Anne Gilchrist seized the pistol from her husband's trembling hand. Unscrewing the silencer free, she handed it to him to put in his pocket. Leave that on the pistol and they would wonder why Baldwin had bothered to use a silencer. Nobody would miss it. She wiped the pistol butt carefully with a cloth before pressing the writer's flaccid hand round it and letting it fall on the carpet. "Watch your feet," she whispered to Gilchrist, indicating a way round the desk to the door. He moved prudently to avoid leaving tell-tale footprints on the bloodstained carpet, or treading on the spattered blood and brains or disturbing the bone splinters. At the door, he swivelled to look back, grimacing with revulsion at the sight. Baldwin lay across the chair where he had slumped when the bullet struck him in the right temple; half his head had gone, torn away by the explosive bullet and his face had contorted out of shape and shrunk; blood welled from his temple and ran down his chest, pooling on the floor. Gilchrist shuddered. He gazed for a moment at his wife. Quite unperturbed, she moved round that grisly body, carrying out her routine with the same clinical detachment he had observed in everything she did, from the hospital to their home. She had planned everything like a chess player. What a woman!

Anne Gilchrist had already typed the note and therefore left the machine as Baldwin had last used it. She propped the envelope on the mantelpiece, then crossed to the door to give a last look round and make sure she had omitted nothing. In the living room, Gilchrist was already tearing up the pages of *A Place to Die*, the manuscript Baldwin kept in reserve against his spells of writer's block. Between them, they shredded and burned half the thick manuscript, scattering the remainder round the room as though the novelist, in a paroxysm of despair, had destroyed his work before killing himself. When they finished, Anne Gilchrist checked everything against the list she had written out. Earlier that week, she had cleaned all her prints off the furniture, glasses and everything else she touched: tonight they had both worn gloves.

"Do you think he was right?" Gilchrist whispered as they put out the living-room lights and stood in the hall. "Do you think this little runt, Quayle, will find out?"

She glanced at him, unable to prevent contempt from hardening the set of her features and her eyes. Sometimes she wondered if he was worth everything she had done for him and the risks she was running. His question did not deserve a reply and she made none. Letting him out of the flat, she stayed there for half an hour in the silent house, with only Baldwin's corpse for company, before making her way home, alone.

22

Harvey Quayle sat unobstrusively at the back of the small coroner's court in Hammersmith, listening to the inquest evidence on Graeme Baldwin. He might have contributed to the proceedings himself, for he had smelled something like self-destruction when he interviewed the jittery and twitchy author just a couple of weeks ago; but he was saving his remarks for Sunday when he would publish a wrap-up of the agency tapes on this inquest, plus his own impressions. No one had the slightest doubt that Baldwin had taken his own life in a fit of depression. Two witnesses referred to his previous suicide attempt and his family doctor affirmed he had treated the novelist for bouts of depressive illness over the years, though not recently. As one of Baldwin's closest friends, his editor and the last man to see the writer before he blew his brains out in his study, Keith Dunning figured as the key witness. Tact sealed his mouth about the real purpose of Baldwin's visit and his brainstorm over the authorship of the Faulds books; in any case, Dunning had too much personal prestige at stake to lose himself in that maze. He contented himself by saying that his author had been suffering from depression and self-doubt for more than a year and during that time had produced nothing when normally he wrote one or two books in that time; he had always suffered badly from the writer's phobia about running out of inspiration and drying up completely.

"So this last note would reflect what you would consider to be his state of mind during that time and particularly in the hours before his death?" asked the coroner, a long, beaky-faced general practitioner. He intoned Baldwin's last note:

"'To Her Majesty's Coroner: For many months I have been unable to work, to fulfil myself through literature. I have been deeply depressed and feel my hold on myself and reality is slipping. Rather than live a diminished existence and one deprived of my abiding passion—literary creation—I have decided to make an end of my life. I hope those few friends whom I respect and who respect me and my work will pardon this gesture because they understand my reasons for it.

"'I leave my literary estate in the capable hands of my friend and editor, Mr. Keith Dunning, and my friend and literary agent, Mr. Harold Seaborne.

"'My books are my real testament. Graeme Baldwin.'"

Dunning looked at the coroner. "That letter would reflect Mr. Baldwin's mental attitude over the past several months," he said.

After the coroner pronounced Baldwin had committed suicide while suffering from depression, the courtroom emptied. In the foyer, Quayle watched the small procession, a scattering of journalists and writers, including a couple of Eddystone Prize jurors. Baldwin's divorced wife, a frosty, painted blonde, walked past with his snooty daughter. Both dry-eyed. For such a famous novelist, how few real friends Baldwin had!

Next day, Quayle's office phone rang. A woman wanted to know if he was the man who had reported on the Liam Faulds mystery. Well, she had studied the *Sunday Herald* pictures and was sure she recognized the face, even though it normally had neither a beard nor glasses. "If it's the same man, his name's Gilchrist and he writes articles for London papers and magazines."

"Where does he live?"

"Chelsea or Fulham, I think. It's his wife I know best. She's at that big hospital near Hammersmith." Her voice had a North Country burr and sounded muffled as though she had a cold. She knew little more about the Gilchrists, and she refused to give her own name, despite Quayle's probing and persuasiveness.

In the *Sunday Herald* library, Quayle consulted various magazine files and read some of Gilchrist's articles. Not a line in those suggested the writer who had created *A Common Grave* and had just finished a novel that literary scuttlebutt whispered would surpass the Ulster story.

Quayle traced the Fulham address; but before tackling Gilchrist, he quizzed the neighbours. Several women scanned both sets of pictures and asserted they were of Gilchrist. He had spent several months away from home that year, for a neighbour looked after his little girl while the mother did her hospital shift. No, nothing indicated they had struck it rich, for they lived modestly and the mother still worked. They were quiet, courteous people, as Irish Catholic as Saint Patrick.

At Charing Cross Hospital, he sought out Mrs. Anne Gilchrist in the surgical wards. She scoffed in his face, then giggled at his suggestion. "If my Martin's Liam Faulds and making all that money they blather about and keeping it to himself and me toiling here six days a week for a pittance, it's myself he'll be reckoning with." She glanced at his pictures, saying they were like thousands of Irish people. "Go and have a look."

"I took these in Belfast."

"That's what I'm after meaning," she came back, and he wondered if she was affecting this Irish double-talk, or if it came naturally.

"I'd like to meet your husband. Is he in London now?"

"So far as I know. If he's not living it up like a millionaire he's working in the Kensington Public Library," she said. "He's doing some research for an article he's writing." As he left, she called after him, "If he's made up that story, let me know."

At Kensington library he had no difficulty identifying Gilchrist from the pictures he had taken, though he could not have sworn he was the man he had encountered in the public lavatory in Belfast. As Anne Gilchrist said, her husband looked like thousands of Irishmen. Gilchrist sat in the reference room surrounded by half a dozen bulky volumes, including *Burke's Peerage* and *Who's Who*. Throwing down his pen, he accused Quayle of making a sick joke when he proposed that he, Martin Gilchrist, was Liam Faulds. Quayle piled fact on fact, citing the neighbours as witnesses, pointing to Gilchrist's trips to Ireland; but the other man refused to cede an inch. "Just because I bear some likeness to those pictures," he protested, tossing the large prints back at Quayle. "It's worse than ludicrous, it's idiotic." When Quayle finally turned to leave, he called after him, "If you dare print anything about me and Faulds in that scandal sheet of yours, I'll sue you for a quarter of a million pounds."

"Make it half a million," Quayle said with a grin. "It's a long time since the paper and I had a really good libel case to give us a circulation lift."

At three-thirty that afternoon, Quayle took post outside the school with the Gilchrists' young woman friend who collected and cared for Moira. He had already introduced himself at Simon Close and now he told her the story that he had arranged with Moira's mother to drive the little girl home and wait there for Anne Gilchrist to finish her hospital duty. When the school came out, Moira spotted them, running across the playground hand-in-hand with the woman's little daughter. Moira needed no pushing to accompany the journalist; for her, it was something novel. Grabbing his hand, she fell into step and headed for the car.

"You haven't seen much of your daddy this year, have you, Moira?"

"He left me and Mummy alone," she said plaintively.

"Where did he go?"

"Mummy made me promise not to say, never ever."

"Was it Ireland?"

She pointed her round face up, giving him a knowing, old-fashioned look. Quayle was conjuring a bag of toffees from a pocket; he unwrapped one, slowly, popped it into his mouth, sucked it, then held out the bag. Moira looked at it, longingly. "Mummy said not to take sweets from anybody, never ever," she said. Then her face split into a grin, she tossed her straight, blond hair and plunged a pudgy hand into the bag; it emerged clutching three caramels. Quayle laughed.

"Did you ever hear your mummy or daddy speak about your uncle, Liam Faulds?"

"He's not my uncle."

"Oh! who is he, then?"

"He only came once. I was in bed. He wrote a book with Daddy and Mummy helped— I think."

"Did you see him?" Quayle had to make an effort to keep his voice neutral. Moira's blond head bobbed up and down in affirmation. "What was he like?"

"Daddy was bigger and better-looking. He had a funny nose. It wasn't straight."

"Moira, how did you know he was called Liam Faulds?"

"I don't know." Her nose wrinkled as she thought about the question. "I just know, that's all," she said.

Quayle hoisted her into the passenger seat, strapped her in and drove through the back streets to Simon Close, quizzing her painlessly as they went. At the house she produced her own key to the front door and led him up the three flights of stairs to the flat. Once inside, she skipped through the L-shaped living room to the kitchen, where she opened the fridge and brought out a bottle of fruit juice, leaving the journalist in the living room. Quayle's gaze tracked slowly

176

round the room with its cheap carpets, curtains and furniture; he looked at the bookshelves with a couple of dozen hardback and paperback books, including the cheap edition of *A Common Grave*. Nothing much there. On the mantelpiece, he saw photo portraits of Gilchrist and his wife with a moon-faced boy who had a vacant, defective look; there was also a studio portrait of Moira. She returned and slurped down her fruit juice through a straw.

"Does Mummy help you with your homework?" he asked and she made that little head-bob signifying yes. "Where? At the table?" Still sucking, she waved her left hand from side to side, then pointed to a desk with a flap top, half-hidden in the dining corner of the living room. Moira crossed the room and pulled open the flap. For a moment, Quayle could not believe his eyes. There, piled before the pigeon-holes and tiny drawers, stood a half dozen exercise books exactly like those Dunning had shown him containing the handwritten version of *A Common Grave*. Quayle had actually photocopied several dozen pages of that book. "Can I see?" he said. Moira nodded, handing him the top book. Quayle flipped open the cover and read the title words in block letters: *The Life and Death of Liam Faulds*. This and the script that followed obviously belonged to the same hand that had copied *A Common Grave*. Nobody could forge that handwriting with its whorls and twists and curlicues. "Moira, I want to take a picture of you. You'd like that, wouldn't you?" Her head bobbed, innocently. He put the exercise book, title page outwards, in her hands and, with his miniature camera, ran off a whole series of snaps showing the title and some of the script with Moira to establish the place; he took shots of her with the portraits of her parents and the mongol child, with her own portrait and against the houses and gardens around the flat. Persuading the child to go and help herself to another fruit juice, he got busy copying the other pages with his camera. He fell on one passage that read:

I must emphasize that the idea of masquerading as Liam Faulds did not start as a game, or even a plot, but as an attempt to feel a human story of love and life and death through another involved person's senses and brain, through the skin and bones even. Gradually the man I had imagined as Liam Faulds became a sort of *alter ego* or *doppelgänger* while I was creating the characters of the book around him and writing both their story and his. When finally I had put together the story of *A Common Grave*, what more natural than to credit Liam Faulds for his part in its inspiration and achievement? Only afterwards, when the press, television and everybody else began either pursuing Liam Faulds or speculating about his background and his motives for remaining an anonymous and mysterious figure, did I realize what a tiger I had grabbed by the tail. Perhaps I should have confessed then. But I did not. Something prevented me. And that small, initial lie built up into a mountain of masquerade and mendacity. To many people it may sound incredible, but I really felt that killing off Liam Faulds would be like killing a part of myself. It was at that moment that the game started to grow serious. . . .

With nearly seventy exposures in his pocket, Quayle took the wondering child's hand and led her downstairs to the woman who normally cared for her. He apologized smoothly, saying his office had contacted him and he had to return urgently. Would she express his gratitude to Mrs. Gilchrist? He would get in touch with her later and thank her personally. Quayle had no intention of alerting Anne Gilchrist to the fact that he had illegally entered her flat and stolen proof that her husband had written *A Common Grave* and invented the fictitious Liam Faulds to cover his own tracks. She might deny the story *after* it had appeared, but he was not going to offer her the chance of denying it *beforehand*. He had another good reason for keeping quiet: she might present or sell it to a rival sheet.

Driving back to his office, Quayle exulted at the idea of throwing all those blown-up pictures of Gilchrist alias Faulds on Jack Gibbon's desk and watching his face. Gibbon would slap him on the back, clear half the front page and a couple of inside pages for a scoop like this. Then he'd want to know how much it cost. What could he demand for a story like this? A thousand quid . . . no, maybe two thousand, or two and a half for palm-oil and all those tip-offs, the spade work, the camera art and everything else. And Gibbon, after a lot of wear and tear on his dentures, would have to chuck in another thousand as a bonus. Funny, how simple the whole thing had been. Yet, Quayle had a strange smell in his long nose of having followed a paper-trail leading him right up to to the jackpot answer. Who was the dame who had phoned? It couldn't possibly have been a pal of Gilchrist and his hard-faced wife, for they disclaimed any part in this literary double-bluff. But maybe they denied it too vehemently. Something about that titian-haired bitch gave him the gears. She reminded him of that housekeeper who had poisoned her wealthy mistress, then her own husband. And Gilchrist? Who'd have imagined an Irish navvy like that could write a best-seller that would eventually become a classic? To Quayle, it smacked of the three monkeys with three typewriters and an eternity who finally churned out the complete Shakespeare. Had that kid of theirs really met the genuine Liam Faulds? Or maybe the mysterious man who did create Faulds? What the hell! He had pushed the story as far as he could. Whatever lay behind that monkey puzzle, he had his scoop and a right humdinger at that. Gilchrist was Liam Faulds. Nobody, and least of all he, Harvey Quayle, should ever kick gift horses in the teeth.

Quayle's story and his series of articles on Liam Faulds caused a sensation and won him the Journalist of the Year award. After publication of his research and the pictures showing the texts of *A Common Grave* and those exercise books recounting the birth and death of Faulds, nobody doubted that Gilchrist was the mystery author. Finally, he and his wife had to confess—though their feigned reluctance fooled even Dunning and convinced Quayle he was right. It had all started, they affirmed, as a serious literary project; but since Martin Gilchrist had never succeeded as a writer under his own name and was attempting a different style, he had launched the book under a pseudonym. He had taken all those complicated steps and made all those trips to Ireland to prevent the publishers from discovering they had already rejected previous works by him. But he had a stronger motive. His story might have inspired the erroneous notion that as an Irish Catholic he had once belonged to the IRA, or still did. Public suspicion and numerous articles stating *A Common Grave* was the work of an IRA man proved his point, Gilchrist asserted. Never at any time had he envisaged the book would run away as it did, or that the Liam Faulds mystery would generate such excitement. Anne Gilchrist said as little as she must; she kept a discreet silence about Quayle's abduction of her daughter and his visit to her flat. He might have grown too inquisitive about that tip-off call and the anonymous note to the *Herald* editor.

Gilchrist negotiated new contracts with Dunning and everyone else involved with *A Common Grave* under his new name. However, he stipulated that his wife should receive half his royalties and rights. For his part, Dunning sometimes wondered about that bizarre conversation with Baldwin the night of the novelist's suicide, and how he knew about the Gilchrists and their second book; but his curiosity stopped a long way short of any action. Perhaps Gilchrist had merely asked Baldwin to touch up his books—and that was his business. To profit from the publicity given to the Faulds revelations everywhere, Dunning rushed the second novel, *An Accident of Birth*, into print. It promised to outstrip even the first Faulds book, which had already made a fortune for the author, his wife and Gresham and Holt. Indeed, there seemed no end to the exploitation of *A Common Grave*. An international film company was spending $20 million to shoot the film on location in Northern Ireland with big-name stars; a play based on the book had already been staged in the provinces and would soon migrate to the West End and

Broadway; there was even an offer that the Gilchrists were considering to turn it into a musical. It would, one cynic observed, finish up as a ballet on ice, underwater and then in space.

As a final irony, the book won the Eddystone Prize. No one disputed its claims. Before the jury voted, Ronald Cranmore, more shrivelled than ever and still dribbling black saliva, rendered a tear-jerking tribute to his former fellow juror, Graeme Baldwin (now safely reduced to ash and bonemeal in the Garden of Remembrance at Hammersmith Crematorium). He felt in his blood that Baldwin would have voted for the Faulds book. It was the sort of book he admired so much and would have liked to write himself. Gilchrist accepted the prize with a brief, modest speech, paying tribute to his predecessors honoured with the Eddystone, among them Graeme Baldwin whom he had always esteemed and would liked to have known.

A year later, Gilchrist published *The Life and Death of Liam Faulds*, last of the Faulds books—a carefully pruned and edited version of the diary written by Baldwin and salvaged from the papers stolen from his cupboard and the bank strongbox. After that, it seemed Liam Faulds suddenly ceased to inspire Martin Gilchrist who, if he published several short stories manifesting little talent and no distinction, never wrote another novel.

Some people doubt Gilchrist's confession; they contend that a man with such a prosaic style, who wrote such dull and trite stories, could never have created any of the three Faulds books. Others go further and believe a person named Liam Faulds did exist but vanished after composing the novels that somehow fell into the hands of Gilchrist and his wife. A few people affirm and continue to affirm, despite the Gilchrists' protestations, that Liam Faulds still lives and will one day appear to claim true authorship of his three books.